The Lit Report

If the characters or theme of this book reminds you of yourself or a friend, don't be afraid to ask for help from a WGSS counsellor.

The Lit Report

SARAH N. HARVEY

Walnut Grove Secondary
School District #35
Langley, BC

ORCA BOOK PUBLISHERS

Library and Archives Canada Cataloguing in Publication

Harvey, Sarah N., 1950-
The lit report / written by Sarah N. Harvey.

ISBN 978-1-55143-905-1

I. Title.

PS8615.A764L58 2008   jC813'.6   C2008-903337-X

First published in the United States, 2008
Library of Congress Control Number: 2008929107

Summary: It will take all of Julia's wit, ingenuity and compassion
to help her best friend through her unexpected pregnancy.

Orca Book Publishers gratefully acknowledges the support for its publishing programs provided
by the following agencies: the Government of Canada through the Book Publishing Industry
Development Program and the Canada Council for the Arts, and the Province of British Columbia
through the BC Arts Council and the Book Publishing Tax Credit.

Design and typesetting by Teresa Bubela
Cover photo by Sarah MacNeill

ORCA BOOK PUBLISHERS
PO Box 5626, STN. B
VICTORIA, BC CANADA
V8R 6S4

ORCA BOOK PUBLISHERS
PO Box 468
CUSTER, WA USA
98240-0468

www.orcabook.com
Printed and bound in Canada.
Printed on 100% PCW recycled paper.

11 10 09 08 • 4 3 2 1

*To Joan, my first reader, who laughed
and cried in all the right places.*

Acknowledgments

Thank you first and foremost to my children, who encourage me, inspire me and provide me with endless material. I am grateful also to my editor, Bob Tyrrell, for his support and expertise; to Teresa Bubela, art director *extraordinaire*, for designing a gorgeous cover; to Dayle Sutherland and Andrew Wooldridge, for their unflagging enthusiasm; and to Christine Toller, for lunchtime debriefs and trips to London Drugs. Susan Eyres, of Cook Street Community Midwives, cheerfully read the manuscript, gave me detailed feedback and answered all my questions about pregnancy, birth and postnatal care. Any remaining errors are entirely my own.

One

Whether I shall turn out to be the hero of my own life, or whether that station will be held by anybody else, these pages must show.

— Charles Dickens, *David Copperfield*

I'm not going to lie to you.

My opening line may not be as brilliant as the opening line of *David Copperfield*, but not many lines are. I adore Dickens. I realize that this is a peculiar and deeply uncool confession from a seventeen-year-old girl, but I can't help that. My book is sort of like *David Copperfield*—it's about parents and children and the abuse of power—but don't freak out and stop reading just because of that. It's not nearly as long as *David Copperfield*, it doesn't have hundreds of characters with weird names, and it's full of sex and foul language. Well, not full, exactly. But there is a bit of both.

Maybe in two hundred years the first line of *The Lit Report* by Julia Riley will be on a test in some futuristic high school where everyone wears identical silver jumpsuits and all lectures are simulcast from a central teaching facility somewhere in rural Saskatchewan. Maybe some things never change and there will always be pop quizzes like the one Mrs. Hopper sprang on us in Lit class last week. There was a lot of groaning when she announced the quiz and even more when she handed out the assignment: *Identify three of the first lines listed below and write a brief paragraph (150–200 words) on the significance of each one.* This was good news for me— I had actually read all five of the books the quotations were taken from—but not so good for many of my classmates, who consider reading a form of punishment.

I finished the quiz quickly and had a lot of time to sit and think about what makes a great first line. I thought about it so much that I wrote an extra mini-essay comparing and contrasting "This is George." and "Call me Ishmael." My thesis was that the first sentence of a novel, whether it's written for four-year-olds or forty-year-olds, sets the tone for the whole book and reveals much of what is to come. It can be two words or twenty or two hundred—it doesn't matter. If the first line doesn't hook the reader, the book is doomed. End of story. Mrs. Hopper gave me bonus points for my essay, accompanied by her trademark happy face with cat's-eye glasses. I wondered if it was possible for a lousy book to have a fabulous first line and whether all great books have great beginnings. And then I started to think about how I would start my own story. And then I decided to try.

So here is my opening sentence again, in case it didn't make an indelible impression on you the first time.

I'm not going to lie to you.

It pissed me off that Ruth ditched me and went alone to Sharon West's party one Saturday night in early November. But when she didn't get on the bus at her stop the following Monday, I started to worry. Especially after I saw the Grim Reaper. I was on the upper level of a red double-decker bus, trying to avoid talking to my classmates. I'm not a morning person so I usually read on the bus, which confirms my reputation as a grind, if not a complete freak. No one on the bus is likely to engage me in conversation about *Jane Eyre* or *The Satanic Verses*, so it works out okay. But that day I had forgotten my book, probably because I was upset with Ruth, and as I gazed out the window, the Grim One zipped across the crosswalk on one of those skinny silver scooters, scythe over one shoulder, cowl casting a deep shadow over his face. Ruth would have enjoyed the vision of Death on a scooter. She certainly wouldn't have assumed, as I did, that it was a bad omen. She would have snorted and said, "Bad omen, my ass. What's next? Jesus on a Segway? Mary in a Smart Car? The Holy Ghost on rollerblades?" My reasoning was that since Halloween had come and gone, the Grim Reaper was a sign and not just a kid in a leftover Wal-Mart costume.

I closed my eyes and listened to the music seeping out of my seatmate's headphones. I inhaled the perfume the girl in front of me had bathed in, wondering idly which cash-crazed celebrity had lent her name to this particularly nasty combination of musk and—was that licorice? I don't wear perfume. It makes me sneeze, and besides, it's frowned upon at my house, along with smoking, junk food, alcohol, drugs, swearing, sex, all forms of popular music and most of the other things normal teenagers take for granted. I have a cell phone, but only because my mother likes to keep tabs on me. Also because she got a great two-for-one deal through her job at the law firm. I'm only supposed to shut it off during school and church or if I'm asleep (which I often am at church or school). When it rang on the bus, I assumed it was just my mom making sure I'd packed the nutritious lunch she left in the fridge for me. She leaves for work before I go to school, but she always puts a note with my lunch, a note that she signs *In God's love,* as if her own love is insufficient to the task.

I reached into my pack and shut the phone off without looking at it. I wasn't up for a lecture on the merits of skin-less chicken breasts. My mother frets about my weight. I was an adorably chubby baby, a cute but chunky little kid, and I'm a pretty hefty teenager, which is neither cute nor adorable. I could easily model for a Botero painting—I'm all ass and thighs. Most of the girls I go to school with are more Giacometti-esque, if that's a word. Not that they'd know what I meant. My mother, who has never weighed a feather over 130 pounds, even when she was pregnant, is a devoted perimeter-aisle shopper and fanatical participator in Christian-themed step-aerobics classes (don't ask). Baked potatoes are a huge indulgence at our house, as is full-fat sour cream, real bacon or any of the other things that make a baked potato even remotely edible. I tease her about worshipping the Canada Food Guide, and if she's in a good mood she swats me with a Beatitudes tea towel. If she's in a bad mood, I get a lecture on sacrilege. She is proud that she has never eaten a Big Mac. I'm pretty sure she believes that heaven is full of anorexic angels, sort of a divine Calvin Klein ad with wings. Maybe she thinks there is a special hell for fat people, and her only child is going to end up there, and we will be separated throughout eternity by my belly flab. She is mystified by my weight and probably prays nightly that my metabolism will self-correct. She doesn't know that for the last four years, ever since I've had an income from babysitting, I've eaten at least one Big Mac a day. More if I have time and money. I also inhale fries, guzzle milkshakes, devour pizza and suck back as much pop as my bladder can stand. I make Queen Latifah look like a wood nymph.

The bus pulled up in front of my school, and I got up and staggered down the narrow spiral staircase and out the back door.

"When's the baby due?" Mark Grange yelled as I made my way up the stairs to homeroom. Mark's a wiry little guy in grade ten, taking every possible liberty with the school uniform: pants slung low so you can see what brand of underwear he wears (Joe Boxer with happy faces), unlaced black oxfords, white shirtsleeves rolled up to his knobby elbows, plaid tie hanging like a scarf around his scrawny neck, blazer stuffed in his pack.

I rubbed my belly and smiled beatifically. Maybe it really was time to start dieting. "Any day now," I said serenely. "Any day." I squeezed myself into my desk as Mr. Dooley's voice came over the PA system, exhorting us to prayer and reminding us that it's hotdog day. Goody—cheap calories. While I listened, I looked over at Ruth's desk. No sign of Ruth, but her lucky hair elastic was sitting where she left it, wrapped around a tin of Altoids (like Ruth, they are curiously strong). A picture of Ruth playing tonsil hockey with Queen Elizabeth is taped to the desk. Ruth's dad has Photoshop on his computer so he can put color pictures—sunrises, rainbows, big-eyed African children—in the programs he makes for his church. He claims people put more in the collection plate if they have something inspirational to look at during his sermon. Ruth has been Photoshopping for years, so she has a great collection of pictures of herself with everybody from Raffi and Big Bird to the Pope and the Dalai Lama. The only thing that the pictures have in common is that all the celebrities, with the exception of Big Bird, look like dwarves, and Ruth looks like an Amazon. I have no idea whether this is intentional or simply a technological glitch.

Ruth has always been big: big-boned, big-headed, big-mouthed, big-hearted, big-haired, big-assed. When I first met her, which was in Sunday school when we were four, she was already taller, broader, louder and wilder than most of the boys in our little class. She would climb on top of our Bible-crafts table and belt out "Jesus loves me" or "What a friend we have in Jesus" at the top of her lungs until one of the lemon-sucking deacons would come running down the stairs from the sanctuary and hiss at Miss Reynolds to keep Ethel Merman quiet. I had no idea who Ethel Merman was, but I was in awe of Ruth, who jumped down from the table, smiled sweetly at Miss Reynolds and said she was just singing for Jesus. When she was older, whenever anyone tried to shut her up, she'd say, "I'm making a joyful noise unto the Lord—is that so wrong?" For some reason—maybe because of my look of abject adoration, or maybe because I gave her my crackers and cheese—Ruth latched onto me that first Sunday and we've been inseparable ever since.

I have a few other friends at school. Brandy Light, who is skinny and pale to the point of invisibility, sits behind me in homeroom. She doesn't have an eating disorder—she's just one of those people who can eat crap all day without gaining an ounce. She loves candy, especially Reese's Peanut

Butter Cups, hates all forms of exercise and loathes the sun.
Brandy has an older brother named Bud, who's in and out
of jail, and twin little sisters named Margarita and Cristall.
It's a good thing their mother found Jesus before she had a
chance to name a kid Highball or Shooter. My mother says
Bud is messed up because every time he says his full name,
people laugh at him. I don't agree. I think Bud is messed
up because his mother drank a case of his namesake every
day she was pregnant with him. No amount of prayer is
going to fix that.

Stewart and Marshall sit on either side of Brandy. Stewart
is Korean and Marshall is Pakistani. For reasons unknown
and unfathomable, they model themselves after Dean Martin
and Jerry Lewis and make terrible jokes about women, Jews
and black people. They insist they're being ironic. Of all of
us, only Brandy believes in God, and even she won't let a
wwjd bracelet touch her bony wrist. What Would Jesus Do
at Westland Christian High School? Turning water into wine
would be frowned upon, as would hanging out with hookers.
And forget about loaves and fishes in the cafeteria. Unless
he could turn them into tuna melts. I figure Jesus would
be happiest hanging out with me and my friends. I just
can't see him playing on the basketball team or joining the
Young Entrepreneur's Club. He might sign up for the choir,
I guess, but is there anything in the Bible about his ability
to carry a tune? At Westland, in order to graduate, you have

to join a club and commit to it for a full school year. Since none of us wanted to join the Bluegrass Club, the Mountain Biking Club, the Future Homemaker's Club or the Forensics Club (although that one sounded kind of cool), Ruth and I formed our own club. The Classics Club is fully sanctioned by the school and devotes itself to the reading and discussion of classic books that have been made into movies or TV shows. We meet once a month at Stewart's house, since he has the biggest TV. Because I've usually read the books, I hand out copies of a brief book report, Brandy fakes some discussion notes, Stewart and Marshall bring the movie, and Ruth provides the food. As we anticipated, no one else has ever tried to join, although if Jesus asked, I guess we'd have to let him in. He might have some interesting things to say about *Madame Bovary* or *The English Patient*.

Basically, Christian school is something that makes our parents feel good. Anyone with half a brain (which is about half the student population) can figure out that we're covering the same curriculum as other high schools—we just have Christian teachers, mandatory Bible study and daily prayer as well. We still have to write math exams, but no one bats an eye if you get down on your knees by your desk and ask for divine assistance. You're actually likely to get a better grade if you do, assuming you don't get caught reading the answers taped to the underside of your desk. In that case, you will be sent directly to Hell (aka Principal Dooley's office).

And don't believe anyone who tells you that kids at Christian schools don't do drugs, drink or have a lot of sex; we're teenagers, for God's sake.

The morning I saw the Soul Snatcher—after Mr. Dooley's announcements and after the obligatory prayer-fest and roll call (Ruth's absence was noted with a bit of eye-rolling on Mrs. Gregory's part)—I applied myself quite diligently to chemistry, physics and geography. It's always easier to concentrate when Ruth isn't around. She's my best friend, but if we had mottos mine would be *Don't Rock the Boat* and hers would be *I Wonder What Capsizing Would Feel Like?* I actually like school, a shameful fact that I reveal to as few people as possible. My grades can't help but reflect my fondness for academic stuff, but I keep my report cards to myself. My mom signs off on them, murmuring "Thank You, Jesus," like he's my extra-special tutor. Report card day at Ruth's house is seldom a happy occasion. Ruth is brilliant, but in a wacky way. She can't do calculus to save her life, but she does a great business in signature forgery. There's a big market for that around report card time. I keep telling her that not graduating from high school will ruin our grand plan, and, to her credit, she's not actually failing anything at the moment. And of course she's never absent without a note signed by one of her parents.

At lunchtime I thought she might turn up at the Dairy Queen, but she wasn't there so I trudged back to school alone with a belly full of the Brownie Batter Blizzard I need to keep me awake during Bible study. At the end of the day, when I finally dug my cell phone out of the bottom of my pack, I found fifteen text messages from Ruth, all saying the same thing: *Call me NOW!* Since the first message had been sent when I was on the bus that morning, I figured I could wait until I got home to call her. Talking to Ruth can be exhausting, and I like to be comfortable while she yammers at me. Plus, I was still a bit pissed off. Somewhere between the Dairy Queen and closing prayers, I'd gotten over worrying that the Reaper was an omen. Ruth's text messages confirmed that she must be okay. Bored, but okay.

When I got home, I picked up the snack my mother had thoughtfully left in the fridge and took it to my room. Baby carrots and broccoli florets—yum. I keep a small cooler in what Ruth calls my hopeless chest, which is her idea of a witty *double entendre*. My hope chest also contains an assortment of salty, fat-laden snack foods and a stack of tea towels embroidered with ironically appropriate Bible verses like "He has filled the hungry with good things and sent the rich away empty." I grabbed a jar of ranch dressing, a Coke and a bag of Doritos, swiped a few carrots through the dressing, nibbled a few chips and burrowed under my duvet to call Ruth. When she answered, I yelled, "Bueller!" in my best Dean Rooney voice. In my opinion, *Ferris Bueller's Day Off* is a classic, even though it wasn't a book first.

Ruth and I quote from it all the time. Maybe she hadn't spent the day driving around in a sports car or leading a parade, but she sure as hell hadn't been suffering through math and Bible study like me.

When she didn't laugh I yelled "Bueller!" again.

"Shut up," she snapped. "It's not like that. I've been here all day, in bed, waiting for my best friend to return my calls."

"Are you sick?" I asked, suddenly feeling guilty for not answering her messages sooner. "Do you have cramps or something?"

"No," she said, "maybe I'll never have cramps again." Even for Ruth, that was a pretty sweeping statement.

"Never have cramps again?" I said. "Cool. Where do I sign up? Did you go to a new doctor?" Ruth and I have been going to the same doctor since we were born. No way would Dr. Mishkin give her anything that affected her reproductive abilities, not without her parents' approval, which they would never give. Not ever. We're supposed to abstain from sex until we marry and then breed like rabbits. Birth control just doesn't enter into it. We're not even supposed to masturbate.

"Shut up," Ruth moaned. "There's no doctor. It's just that…" Her voice trailed off. She actually sounded sick, and I was getting more worried by the second. Maybe I'd dismissed the Reaper too quickly.

"Just that what?" I said, sitting up in bed and creating an avalanche of chips and carrots.

"I did it," she muttered.

"Did what?"

"It," she said. "You know—sex. I had sex with Rick Greenway. On Saturday night. At Sharon's party. In the upstairs bathroom."

"You had sex with Rick Greenway on Saturday night at Sharon's party in the upstairs bathroom?" I sounded like I was playing *Clue*.

"That's what I said, didn't I?" Ruth was starting to sound less like a character from *Steel Magnolias* and more like my old friend. "What are you, a fucking parrot? We got loaded and we had sex and then I came home. And that's about all I remember. So I can't even tell you if it was any good. My first time and I didn't even get a good look at his dick, so don't ask."

"I wasn't going to," I said, although I couldn't help thinking about it—Rick's dick. Rick's prick. And I didn't even like the guy. I knew that Ruth had vowed not to be a virgin when she entered grade twelve, so she was right on track, if not a little early. "You weren't raped, were you?" I asked.

"Don't be an asshole, Julia. Of course I wasn't raped. I went to the party to get laid and I did. It's just..." Her voice trailed off again.

"What?"

"It's not all it's cracked up to be, that's all. It hurt and it was over really fast."

"Yeah," I said. "I've read about that—you know—in novels."

Ruth snorted. "Yeah, I bet *Pride and Prejudice* is full of stuff about dumb chicks who get drunk and give it up at parties to grade twelve guys with small pricks."

"How small are we talking about?" I asked, looking speculatively at a baby carrot on the floor. She'd obviously seen something. "Zucchini? Parsnip? Dill pickle?" There was a moment of silence. I wondered if Ruth had hung up on me. She does that a lot.

Suddenly there was a loud cackle of laughter from my phone. "Gherkin," Ruth announced. "Definitely a gherkin. With a side order of pearl onions."

"Wow!" I said. "Excellent image. Makes him sound like the deli special."

"Yeah, well, he wasn't."

"Wasn't what?"

"Special. He wasn't special at all." Ruth sounded like she was going to cry again, so I said the first thing that came into my head, something my mom had first said to me when I was thirteen and had a massive unrequited crush on Brandon Portland.

"There's someone special out there for you, sweetie," I said in my suckiest voice.

"Yeah, right," she muttered.

"You deserve at least a Polski Ogorki," I said. "Or maybe you'd prefer a plain old kosher dill—"

"Shut up," Ruth yelled. "You'll be lucky if you get a pickled green bean."

Two

It was the best of times, it was the worst of times, it was the age of wisdom, it was the age of foolishness…

—Charles Dickens, *A Tale of Two Cities*

Don't worry. I'm not going to start every chapter with a Dickens quote. Even I'm not that much of a nerd. But you have to admit, *A Tale of Two Cities* has an awesome first line. Most people have heard "It was the best of times, it was the worst of times" even if they've never read the book. What they don't know is that the sentence goes on and on for over a hundred words. *Over a hundred words.* There's no way that Mrs. Hopper would have let old Charles get away with that. No happy faces for him. Anyway, in just over a hundred elegant words, Dickens gets the point across that it's a good idea to look at things from as many angles as possible, since each person has a unique point of view. Or as my Nana used to say, "There's more than one way to skin a cat." Maybe that's oversimplifying it a bit. Maybe "One man's meat is another man's poison," another of Nana's favorites, is more appropriate. She and Charlie D. would have been soul mates, although, now that I think about it, all her favorite sayings are pretty gruesome. Like, "Living is like licking honey off a thorn." Gross. True, but gross. *A Tale of Two Cities* also has a really famous last line, but that's a whole different thing.

Everything went back to normal after Ruth told me about the party. She didn't mention Rick Greenway (or his tiny tackle) again, and I didn't ask for more details. I informed my mother that I could no longer eat anything pickled. When she asked why, I said it was something to do with deli food being unclean. When my mother became a Christian, which was when I was about three, she immediately joined a Christian book club, the aforementioned exercise class, a group that does devotional ikebana and a choir that sings only Christian country music. She's backed off a bit since then—she dropped the choir and the book club—but she's still so busy that she's never actually gotten around to reading the whole Bible, so she believes just about anything I tell her. Like when I didn't want to go to camp, I told her that, according to the prophet Jeremiah, log cabins were an abomination in the eyes of the Lord. Or when I didn't want to take saxophone lessons, I told her that the playing of brass instruments was expressly forbidden by the Maccabees. I think that one's actually true. Especially when it comes to the tuba.

Ruth doesn't have much luck when it comes to parents. For one thing, she lives with both her parents; I live with just my mom. My dad lives across town with his new wife, Miki, and he's only been to church once that I know of in the past seventeen years. Ruth's parents are certifiable religious lunatics; my mom is a legal secretary who speaks three languages (English, French and Italian), loves musicals and is famous for her Holy Trinity flower arrangements made out of irises, pussy willows and wisps of sphagnum moss. My dad is a nurse in the neonatal unit at the hospital where his wife is a pediatrician. Ruth's father is a preacher, her mom is a preacher's wife and Ruth says that what they don't know about the Bible could fit in a flea's asshole. My mom stopped going to Ruth's dad's church when she realized what a redneck jerk he is. She's never come right out and said it, but that's my interpretation of her switch from the Glory Alleluia Gospel Assembly (aka GAGA) to her current church, All Saints. She says the music's better at All Saints, but I think what she really likes is that Father Shortwell doesn't yell, "I'm in the business of saving souls for Jesus, and my business needs backers," when he passes the collection plate.

Ruth's dad, or Pastor Pete as his parishioners call him, has some dandy tattoos left over from his days behind bars. And I don't mean he was a bartender. The tattoos are all sort of blurry and dreary—knives and hearts and women's names and an awesome Jesus dripping blood from a crown of thorns. Jesus looks suspiciously like Pete's old cellmate, a biker named Two-Percent (because he's not homo). Two-Percent has been a deacon at GAGA since his release five years ago. Peggy is always nagging Pete to have his tattoos lasered off, but Pete loves to "let the tatts testify," as he puts it, although the older he gets, the grosser the testifying gets. But you'd be surprised how many women with big hair and giant boobs join his church after an encounter with Pastor Pete's body art.

IN EARLY DECEMBER, Ruth got sick and missed a few days of school. One Friday morning, Peggy called to ask me to bring Ruth's homework over after school. Peggy still doesn't understand that under no circumstances will Ruth do homework on the weekends. But of course I didn't argue. I rarely argue with adults. It seems like such a waste of energy. In my view, childhood and adolescence are non-negotiable sentences. There is no appeal process. No time off for good behavior, no parole. You might as well just wait it out, make plans for your release and try not to piss off the wardens and the other inmates. It wasn't hard for me to maintain a reputation for quiet piety; I'm smart, I like volunteering at the hospital and recycling my pop cans, and most of my elders are tolerable people. Pretending to be God-fearing was slightly more challenging, but I managed that mostly by keeping my mouth shut and going to church once a week with my mom.

It was a constant source of annoyance to Peggy that I, an only child and the product of a broken home, was much better adjusted than either of her children. To hear Peggy tell it, Ruth has been in trouble since she was in the womb, what with the morning sickness, the premature delivery, the colic, the croup, the broken arm, the eczema, the night terrors, etc., etc. Ruth's older brother, Jonah, was sent to a bible college in northern Alberta right after he graduated high school. Jonah isn't like Ruth. He doesn't smoke, drink or hang around with evil-doers. Jonah's crimes are cultural. He loves music, especially jazz and opera. He reads a lot of philosophy books and claims to be an existentialist. He bought himself a subscription to *Gourmet* magazine with his paper-route money when he was twelve. Which means, according to Pete and Peggy, that Jonah is gay and thus in mortal danger of eternal damnation. I know from personal experience that Jonah is definitely not gay. I've known since I was fourteen and he was sixteen and we fooled around a bit (okay, a lot) on a school camping trip. So Jonah got sent to Bible boot camp, where he's supposed to be scared straight by bad food, worse music and mandatory participation in team sports. It won't work. Jonah knows how to wait it out too. And besides, he's already straight.

The Lit Report

When I got to Ruth's house on Friday afternoon, Pete was putting up Christmas decorations on the front lawn. Even though it was pretty cold out, he was wearing a tight, white, short-sleeved, V-neck T-shirt and no jacket. I could see the spider web tattoo on his left elbow and the skull on his right forearm and a thorn or two of Christ's crown peeking out of his chest hair. I was glad it wasn't July. July means tank tops.

"Hey, Julia," he said, gesturing toward the grotesque inflatable nativity scene he was assembling. "Whaddaya think? She's a beauty, eh?"

"Sure, Mr. Walters," I said. "It's a marvel of ingenuity." I knew he wouldn't want to hear that the wise men, especially Balthazar, looked like sand-weighted drag queens, or that the Baby Jesus could use a little more air.

"You should see it lit up, baby. Once I get the star on the roof—Praise Jesus! People will drive by and stop their cars and get out and fall on their knees!"

"Sure, Mr. Walters," I said again. Fall on their knees laughing, I thought.

"Be sure and come by some night," he said, turning back to pumping up the Virgin Mary. "Bring your mom. I miss her pretty face at the church."

"Sure, Mr. Walters," I said for the third time as I went up the front stairs and rang the doorbell. It played the first few notes of "Stand Up, Stand Up for Jesus." I shivered, but not from the cold.

Peggy opened the door and greeted me with her usual warmth and charm. Peggy always smells as if she's bathed in Mr. Clean.

"Oh, it's you, Julia. Go on up."

"Thanks, Mrs. Walters. That's a lovely apron." I know better than to call her Peggy to her face.

But she had already turned and was halfway to the kitchen before I started up the stairs to Ruth's room. I've been in Ruth's house so many times that I don't even notice anymore how weird it is that the downstairs is immaculate and the upstairs looks as if the Hell's Angels are having a sleepover. I guess the fact that Two-Percent was living in Jonah's room didn't help. Pete and Peggy's spotless bedroom and gleaming en suite bathroom was downstairs in the clean zone. Ruth's room was okay, though. Kind of dark, due to scab-colored curtains, and a bit smelly, due to the incense Ruth burns to cover up other smells, but still strangely cozy.

Ruth had been decorating her room ever since she could hold a crayon, use a pair of scissors and jab a pushpin into drywall. She never takes anything off the walls, so her room is a giant collage. She calls it Installation One: Childhood, and she says that when she leaves home she's going to rip everything down and burn it in the backyard incinerator. I hope she doesn't. There are pictures of us at Bible camp underneath our grade five report about tree frogs; there's Jonah's recipe for key lime pie, a ticket stub from the first

movie we ever went to (*Babe*) and a signed photograph of
Billy Bob Thornton. Every time I go to Ruth's there's something new on the walls. Today it was a lacy Day-Glo orange
thong, splayed on the wall like a giant butterfly.

Ruth was lying in bed reading *People* magazine. On her
night table was a yellow plate with toast crusts on it; beside
the plate was a can of ginger ale. Beside the bed was an
empty plastic ice-cream bucket. Ruth's hair, which she had
recently dyed blue, was pulled back in a ponytail, and she
was wearing red- and white-flowered pajamas. Her face was
very pale.

I giggled and Ruth frowned. "Don't laugh at me.
I puked on my T-shirt," she said, pointing at the pajamas.
"Peggy made me put these on. They suck but at least they
don't stink."

I put Ruth's homework on her desk next to her
computer. The screensaver was a flying monkey from *The
Wizard of Oz* with the words *When monkeys fly out of my
butt* instead of a tail.

"You feeling any better?" I asked, making myself
comfortable in the desk chair and keeping my distance
from Ruth's puke-germs. There's nothing I hate more than
puking. Vomiting scenes in movies make me nauseous.
Even the sight of the bedside bucket made me queasy.

"A bit," Ruth replied. "For a while this morning I thought
I was gonna die, but it's better now. Now I'm just bored.

I can't even be bothered to watch shitty TV. My energy level is, like, zero. No, it's more like negative ten." Ruth pulled her hair out of its elastic and sighed. "Plus, I feel all, kinda, emotional. This morning I cried watching *Regis and Kelly* with my mom. There was something about little homeless kids in Thailand and I just lost it. Plus, my boobs hurt. Like before my period."

"You think you're PMS-ing?" I asked cautiously. If she was, I wasn't going to hang around. A while ago, Ruth had thrown a stiletto-heeled boot at my head when I wouldn't hand over the remote. Other girls get irritable and weepy before their periods; Ruth gets psychotic. I had to have three stitches in my forehead after the boot episode. I scratched the bump where the scar was. Was it really only a month ago? It seemed longer. A lot longer.

"Um, Ruth," I said cautiously. "You've had a period, right? Since, you know, Rick."

Ruth looked at me as if I was insane. "Duh," she said. "You remember. Pizza Day. You freaked out 'cause I took your last tampon. And then the next day your period started and you had to get a pad from the school nurse." She took a sip of ginger ale and belched loudly.

"Yeah, but—" I hesitated, wondering if she would figure it out on her own or if she was just in massive denial. Even Ruth can count to twenty-eight, but this was the first time she'd needed to. "Pizza Day was in October. November was hot dogs." I pulled my agenda out of my pack, opened it and held it out to her. "Look. Pizza Day—October 18. Hot Dog Day—November 16. Remember?" Ruth took one look at the agenda, threw it across the room, leaned over the side of the bed and puked into the ice-cream bucket.

When she was finished puking (it was mostly dry heaves, thank goodness) she started crying, and I left the desk chair and got her a damp washcloth and a glass of water from the bathroom. I curled up on the bed with her and stroked her blue hair away from her sweaty forehead. That's what my mom does when I'm sick and it always helps. I decided against asking her whether they had used condoms. It seemed like locking the barn door after the horse is gone, as Nana likes to say.

When she finally stopped sobbing, I wiped her face with the washcloth and got her to sip some water. I had the idea, even then, that hydration was important.

"I am so fucked," she moaned.

"Well, yeah," I said. "We've established that."

She glared at me and took another sip of water. "It's not funny, Julia. I mean, what am I gonna do? Pete and Peggy will kill me. Or send me away. Look what they did to Jonah, and his biggest sin was listening to Miles Davis." Ruth gulped and reached for the bucket again. I looked away while she retched.

"What about Rick?" I asked.

"What about him?"

"Are you going to tell him? That he's going to be a father?"

Ruth lay down and pulled the pillow over her head so her next words were muffled. It sounded as if she said, "I don't know."

"You don't know?" I repeated.

She sat up suddenly, her face flushed, her hands balled into fists. "I don't know whether he's the father, okay? We were really drunk and a couple of his friends were in the room with us, and I think I did it with at least one other guy, but I don't know who. So, to answer your question, no, I won't be telling Rick. Or my parents. Or Jonah. Or anyone else." Her eyes filled with tears again, and she disappeared under the covers. I could hear her sobbing, but I left her alone. I needed to think.

When we were about ten, Ruth and I had gotten into the habit of making all our decisions with the aid of a piece of ruled stationery with a wavy line drawn down the middle—pros to the left, cons to the right. Oh Henry! or Mars bar. Swimming or biking. Red shorts or blue. We were the Solomons of fifth grade, and by high school we were positively Delphic. Our classmates consulted us on everything. Is it okay to liberate cash from your mother's purse? Absolutely not. Mothers, in our experience, cataloged everything in their purses—tampons, money, breath mints, lipstick. Should you have sex with your best friend's brother? Probably not, although my objectivity was compromised by the huge crush I had on Jonah. Left to our own devices, Ruth made disastrous decisions and I made boring ones. But the paper oracle never let us down as long as we did it together.

Ruth was in no condition to help, so I grabbed some paper out of her printer and started without her. I knew from experience that it wouldn't be long before she would get bored under the covers. One of the great things about Ruth is that she has a moth-flame relationship with catastrophe. She is more than a Drama Queen—she is a Drama Empress. Another great thing is that she's really creative, and I'm really pragmatic, so between the two of us we can usually figure something out. I started with the facts.

Ruth was pregnant. I was pretty sure about that, but I wrote down *Home Pregnancy Test?* anyway. Under *PRO* I wrote *Know for sure.* Under *CON* I wrote *Where to buy? False results? Cost?* and *Know for sure.* The *Know for sures* canceled each other out, which left zero pros and three cons. I could always use my Big Mac money to go across town to a big chain drugstore and buy the test. And the false result thing was mostly about false negatives anyway. I was pretty sure we didn't need to worry about that. Ruth was still snuffling, so there was no one to argue with my logic. Next I wrote *Father?* Then I crossed it out. I didn't think I'd win that argument.

Underneath that I wrote the word *Abortion*. I sat and stared at it until Ruth surfaced. She wandered off to the bathroom, and when she got back I saw that she had washed her face and brushed her hair and put on some mascara. It was safe to say the crying was over.

One good thing about being at Ruth's is that her mom never sticks her head in the door and asks what you're doing or whether you'd like something to eat or drink. That happens a lot at my house. Ruth's parents leave her alone with her phone and her computer, which Pete checks every once in a while for evidence of skanky surfing. If he ever finds anything really raunchy, he yells at her and shuts her down for a few days. Ruth is pretty stealthy when it comes to computers. She knows how to hide her tracks. Unlike her dad, who watches porn on her computer when she's at school. Ruth says that bit of information may come in handy some day.

She sat down next to me and looked at what I'd written. Then she grabbed the pen and paper away from me, scribbled for a few seconds and handed it back. Under *Abortion* she had written *Pro = It's My Life* and *Con = Eternal Damnation*. Ruth doesn't mess around with the paper prophet. I could have added to the list, but I already knew which way we were headed.

Three

There was no possibility of taking a walk that day.

—Charlotte Brontë, *Jane Eyre*

I first read *Jane Eyre* when I was eleven and in my Brontë phase. I devoured all the Brontë girls—Emily, Anne, Charlotte—one November when I had the flu. I briefly adored *Wuthering Heights,* which also has a pretty great first line, but plain Jane eventually won me over. Catherine and Heathcliff are such useless twits. The most famous line from *Jane Eyre* doesn't come until the last chapter, which begins "Reader, I married him." How great a line is that? Not "Reader, he married me." Big difference. But back to the first line. What's a girl to do when she can't go for a walk? When her choices are limited? When everything seems hopeless? She can, like countless heroines of bad literature, find a man to save her or, like Jane, she can work on her other options. And maybe get the guy in the end. I love

Jane Eyre. It's got everything: a smart brave heroine, a flawed hero, true love and a madwoman in the attic. All eleven-year-old girls should read it, but they don't. They're too busy shopping and downloading movies. They won't be as ready as I was for the madwoman.

On Friday morning I told my mom I was going to the downtown library after school to do research for a biology paper. It wasn't a total lie. I really was going to go to the library, but my research wasn't into the kind of biology that's on the school curriculum. I always try and tell interesting lies that contain a grain of truth—not too much detail, plausible, easy to remember. I went online at the library and printed out information about abortions and where to go to talk to someone about getting one. I couldn't risk using the computer at home. My mom isn't suspicious like Pastor Pete, but we live in a tiny apartment—my mom sleeps on a pullout couch—and we share the computer in the living room. We could probably afford a bigger apartment if my mom wasn't supporting about ten African AIDS orphans and donating (or tithing, as she calls it) a percentage of her income to a shelter downtown for battered women. I wished I could talk to Miki or my dad about Ruth's problem—Miki's a baby doctor, after all, and he's a baby nurse—but it was too risky. It would have been a relief to talk to an adult, especially a smart adult with specialized medical knowledge. Miki's a bit brisk, but I've gotten used to her. My mom hasn't.

After my trip to the library, I picked up a home pregnancy test at the downtown London Drugs. The clerk looked at me kind of funny when she scanned it, but home pregnancy tests aren't like cigarettes or booze—you don't have to show ID to get them. I smiled brightly and told her to have a nice day. She said, "You too," and that was it.

As soon as I got to Ruth's, she grabbed the drugstore bag from me and disappeared into the bathroom. While I waited for her to come out, I looked at the most recent additions to her installation. Next to the orange thong was a condom, still in its wrapper, and a Bad Religion CD. I assumed these items were commemorative; I hoped I would have something slightly more romantic to show for my first time. A flower, maybe, or a poem. After a while she came back to her room, shoved the drugstore bag at me, threw herself face down on her bed and yelled, "Fuck, fuck, fuck, fuck, fuck," into her pillow. I didn't really need confirmation, but I fished around in the bag and found both tests—both used, both showing a pink stripe. Big surprise. One more reason for Ruth to hate pink. I buried the bag at the bottom of my pack and waited, pleating into fans the pages of information I'd printed out for her at the library.

Eventually Ruth sat up and said, "This is bad. This is so bad." Her face was all blotchy, and her lips were cracked and sore looking.

"Yup," I said.

"I mean, this is, like, the worst. I keep thinking that it's going to go away, but it's not. Whatever I do—it's not going away—ever. Not if I have an abortion. Not if I give it up for adoption. Not if I keep it." Ruth's voice rose to a wail, and I reached over and turned on her stereo to mask the sound of her grief. Because that's what it was—grief. Any decision she made would lead to more grief—or eternal damnation if Pete and Peggy were to be believed. I wondered again why she hadn't used a condom, but again I didn't ask. I didn't need another visit to the clinic for stitches. Ruth's PMS episodes were formidable enough. I hated to think what pregnancy would do to her moods.

I handed Ruth the fans I'd made and listened to Coldplay while she smoothed out the pages and read all the stuff about manual vacuum aspiration and dilation and evacuation—stuff that had made me feel kind of queasy when I read it, and I wasn't the one who was pregnant. I tried to imagine how she felt. Trapped. Confused. Angry. Sad. Helpless. Maybe even a tiny bit excited. When she had finished reading, she crumpled the pages into a big ball and threw it at me, which I felt was a bit unfair. I know what I felt at that moment. Confused. Angry. Sad. A tiny bit envious and a tiny bit excited. But not helpless. And not trapped.

"There's no way. I can't do it," she said, squeezing her lower lip between her thumb and forefinger. A droplet of blood appeared on a crack in her lip.

"Okay," I said. "No one said you had to. It was just an option. You know, a choice."

"A shitty choice," she muttered, still squeezing.

"If you say so," I said.

"Well, I do," she said. "And not just because of the burning in hellfire thing, either. I mean, I don't really believe that shit, you know I don't. But it still seems…wrong."

I turned the music down. Now that Ruth had downgraded from wailing to moaning, I didn't want Peggy storming in, demanding that we listen to the Oakridge Boys. Not with a drugstore bag full of used pregnancy tests and a big ball of information about abortions in the room.

"Okay," I said, taking my shoes off and crawling onto Ruth's bed. "Here's the deal. You're down to two choices: having the baby and keeping it or having the baby and giving it up for adoption, right?"

Ruth stared at me, her red-rimmed brown eyes wide. "If I keep it, I'll have, like, no life. So I have to give it up, don't I? Right, Julia? I have to give it up."

I knew Ruth better than to try and tell her what to do. "Keeping it doesn't seem like a great idea to me," I replied. "I mean, can you imagine being one of those teenage welfare moms, taking your baby to the free clinic, hanging around the park, smoking and talking about your badass boyfriend. No education, no future." I shuddered. "No thanks. Do you really want that? Don't you want to graduate and move away from here like we planned? And do you really think you're ready to be a mom?"

Ruth was silent for a minute. I could hear Two-Percent blowing his nose in the next room. Gross. "I guess not," she finally said. "I can't even look after a hamster, let alone a baby. Remember what happened to Morton?"

I nodded. Morton the hamster had died when Ruth left him on his own in the backyard. We never found his body—only a sad little pile of hamster fluff. Ruth told her parents that she had witnessed a hamster rapture. Morton had ascended to the sky in a shaft of golden light, she said, even though we had both seen an eagle circling the trees near her house that day. She never had another pet. Now was not the time to start.

"So you're left with your other option, right? Having the baby and giving it up. Which has its own problems. Pete and Peggy will send you away for sure, and we don't want that."

Ruth shook her head vehemently. "No way. I'm not going to some Bad-Girl Bible camp. But what can I do? They're gonna freak. You know that. And there's nowhere else for me to go."

"I know," I said. "But I think there's another way. I thought of this on the bus coming back from downtown. I'm pretty sure it'll work." Ruth nodded and sniffled and wiped her nose on her Holly Hobbie bedspread.

"You know how you hear about girls who give birth on prom night in the girl's washroom and leave the baby in the garbage and no one even knew they were pregnant?"

Ruth nodded again.

"Well, I figure that if you don't gain a lot of weight and you dress in sweats or something, we can hide your pregnancy. And after the baby's born we'll take it to your dad's church and make sure someone finds it, and then it'll be adopted and no one but you and me will ever know. And you won't get sent away and we can finish high school and get outta Dodge, just the way we planned." When I finished speaking, I was as out of breath as when I have to run around the track for PE class. Ruth was staring at me as if I had grown a third breast.

"Are you fucking nuts?" she hissed. "This isn't some dumb movie-of-the-week. I'm pregnant. I'm going to get as big as a vw bug. I'm going to give birth. And it ain't gonna be quiet, I can tell you that right now."

I interrupted her before she could come up with more objections.

"I know all that. Just listen to me. I did a lot of reading today at the library. Not only is it possible to conceal a pregnancy, it's also possible to have a baby without going to a hospital. Lots of women do that by choice these days. They hire midwives so they can have their babies at home. Miki talks about that all the time—how women have to be careful and choose a good midwife and go to the hospital right away if there are any complications. But most of the time it's okay. And you wouldn't believe how many babies are delivered by taxi drivers or pilots or the baby's father. I can do better than that. There are tons of books I can read. I can find out about nutrition and I can teach myself how to do checkups and everything. You know how I love a big research project. This one just won't be for extra credit." I grinned and poked her leg with my toe.

Ruth snickered and absently rubbed her stomach.

"I'm bigger already," she moaned.

"No, you're not," I said. "You just think that because you're lying around all day obsessing about it. The first thing you have to do is get up, get dressed and try to act normal." I looked around at the walls in Ruth's room and thought about the inflatable scene on the front lawn. "Or what passes for normal here."

"Then what?" she asked. I could tell she was warming to the idea already. She could see that I was offering her a chance to crawl out the bathroom window of her life.

"Then you do everything I tell you to do." I laughed. "That'll be a first."

We sat in silence for a moment. I could hear Peggy yelling at Pete, and I heard Two-Percent's motorcycle start up. I could hear Ruth's breathing. She still sounded stuffed up.

"Okay," she said. "What do I do first?"

"First, you have to agree to let me name the baby. Even if you're not going to keep it, I get to name it."

"Sure." Ruth shrugged. "It doesn't make any difference to me. Name it anything you like. Beelzebub would be awesome. Then what?"

"Then I figure out what to do about the morning sickness so you can go back to school on Monday. Then I buy a stethoscope and some vitamins and you stop eating crap."

That got her attention. "But that's all we ever eat around here. Peggy can't cook—you know that."

It was true. Peggy knew everything there was to know about cleaning, but her idea of good nutrition was extra coleslaw with the bucket of KFC. The only time Ruth ate a balanced meal was when she came to my house. I was pretty sure my mom would notice if she started eating all her meals with us.

Ruth continued. "I don't know how to cook. And there's no way Peggy's gonna listen when I say I want organic greens or some other gourmet shit. And have you thought about how much it's gonna cost—all this good nutrition?"

I swung my legs over the side of the bed and reached for my shoes. I was beginning to feel a bit annoyed with Ruth. I knew she was upset, and I was willing to overlook the occasional hormonal outburst, but I thought I'd come up with a pretty good plan, and she was already shooting it down. Without my help, Peggy and Pete would discover her little secret sooner or later, and then where would she be? On a bus to the Home for Knocked-Up Nitwits, that's where. The least I'd expected was a tiny bit of gratitude and maybe a smidgen of cooperation.

"I'm not asking you to do much, you know," I said, getting up from the bed. "Just watch what you eat—I'll even read up about prenatal nutrition and tell you how. Who knows? You might even like it. You're always bitching about your weight. For now, get cleaned up and go get yourself a salad at McDonald's. No dressing." Ruth groaned. "I gotta go. I've got work to do. I'll call you later." I slung my pack over my shoulder and walked out the door.

As I went down the path to the sidewalk, Pete turned on the lights on the Christmas scene, and the biggest, ugliest plastic star I'd ever seen glared down from the top of the house, illuminating the sorry scene below. A helpless unexpected baby. A poor ignorant young mother. The irony was not lost on me.

I looked up at Ruth's window and saw her standing there, watching me leave. I pointed to the scene on the lawn, mimed sticking my finger down my throat and blew her a kiss. She smiled and blew one back. She might be a giant pain in the ass sometimes, but she was my best friend, and besides, she was the one who was pregnant. Whatever else happened in the next little while, I knew it wouldn't be my breasts that would be sore, my stomach that would have stretch marks, my skin that would break out, my bladder that would leak, my ankles that would swell and my vagina that would have to stretch. I didn't have something growing inside me. I had it easy.

Four

It is a truth universally acknowledged, that a single man in possession of a good fortune, must be in want of a wife.

—Jane Austen, *Pride and Prejudice*

When I first read *Pride and Prejudice*, I was only ten, so it's not surprising that I didn't immediately get the irony of that first sentence. I thought it simply meant that it was easy for a rich man to get a wife. Which, ironically, is perfectly true. I mean, all you have to do is look at a few magazines to know that there's nothing easier for a rich man. As easy as buying a Mercedes SUV or jetting off to a private resort on the Turks and Caicos for the weekend. If one wife doesn't work out, well, there's always another one—usually a younger one—coming down the pike. It took a few readings before I realized that *Pride and Prejudice* wasn't all about romance, although it's just as romantic as *Jane Eyre*, maybe more so. Anyway, after I figured out what irony was and wasn't (no thanks to you, Alanis Morissette), I really started to appreciate *P & P*. I've tried to convince Ruth that Jane Austen wrote chick lit long before Bridget Jones came along, but the only similarity Ruth sees is that Colin Firth was in both movies. What she actually said was, "Why should I read about people with poles up their butts when I have you?" I shut her up by telling her that sarcasm is irony's redneck cousin. Well, at least I have a cousin, was her reply. Which is true and stupid and neither ironic or sarcastic. Strange as it sounds, *P & P* helped me understand why my dad left my mom and why he and Miki are together. He is Miki's good fortune and she is his, even though at first he was prejudiced against her because she was a rich doctor, and she was too proud to see that a scruffy singing nurse was just what she needed.

After I left Ruth's that Saturday, I took the bus over to my dad's and let myself in. I go and visit Dad every weekend. That's been the arrangement ever since he moved out when I was five. At first I went to his crappy little bachelor apartment a couple of blocks away, and then he moved to an equally crappy one-bedroom condo out near the hospital. Now I go to the five-bedroom art deco house he and Miki bought after they got together. I bet Miki made the down payment. A nurse—especially a child-support-paying nurse—wouldn't even be able to cover the payments on the garage. It's a beautiful house; every room but one has an ocean view. That one room is what they call the decompression chamber. It's tiny and narrow and you reach it by going up a little staircase tucked in the corner of the front hall. It's sort of like being in a boat that never leaves the wharf. There's a big porthole instead of a window, and a built-in berth where you can read or sleep or stare out the window at an arbutus tree. It's always just the right temperature and there's no TV, no radio, no phone. There's even a *Do Not Disturb* sign to hang on the doorknob if you don't want to be called for meals or phone calls. No one is allowed to stay all night in the chamber—it's strictly for short-term use—and sometimes we fight over it (isn't that ironic?), but it's my favorite room in the house when I have things to think about. I planned to get in there soon.

I sleep over at my dad's every Friday and Saturday night. On Sunday morning my mom picks me up and we go to church, and then I go back to my dad's and we have brunch and he returns me to my mom's on Sunday night after dinner. Church attendance is non-negotiable. It's a complicated arrangement, but it's the only deal my mom would make. Take it or leave it. My dad took it. Every now and again Mom will ask me if I want to alter the arrangement, but since I don't, that's about the extent of our discussions. Mom starts stiffening up on Friday afternoon, and by the time my dad drops me off on Sunday, she looks like she's taken a bath in a vat of starch. She and my dad are polite to each other, but you can tell that, even after more than ten years, just seeing him makes her feel shitty. She won't talk about him with me; she never has. Not a word. It's a bit creepy. Sometimes I think it might be easier if they weren't so civilized, if they yelled at each other and called each other *bitch* and *asshole* and stormed around the house throwing dishes and slamming doors. It makes me wonder if there ever was any passion between them, and if not, how I was conceived. Politely, I guess. May I touch? Yes, please, by all means. Thank you. You're welcome. Good night.

My dad met Miki at the hospital a few years ago, and they got married last year on Maui. My mom let me go to the wedding, but only after my dad promised to take me to church on the one Sunday we were there. The whole thing was pretty cool—even the church part, which was simultaneously exotic (the choir wore really loud muumuus) and familiar (Say amen, somebody!). I discovered that singing "Just a Closer Walk with Thee" is tolerable when you're wearing a sundress and flip-flops and you know you're going to go surfing later and buy fresh papayas for lunch. My dad sang all the hymns and clapped and swayed as if he'd temporarily forgotten that he left my mother partly because she believed in what he called "a complete pile of horseshit." I don't think Miki was overjoyed to suddenly be the stepmother of a teenage girl, but she's so busy it hardly makes any difference to either of us. If she's around, she hangs out with us, but sometimes I think she arranges to work more weekends than she has to. We don't kid ourselves. I already have a perfectly good mother.

My dad had told me that Miki would be working, so I was surprised to see her red Mini Cooper in the driveway next to my dad's dark green Honda. Early in December, I had helped my dad put up the Christmas lights—tiny white ones—on the branches of the arbutus tree in the front yard. It was festive, yet understated.

"Hello," I yelled as I dropped my pack on the slate tiles in the front hall. No reply. I slipped off my boots and wandered down to the kitchen. "Anybody home?" I snagged a banana out of the fruit bowl and continued my reconnaissance as I ate it. "Where are you guys?"

"Up here." My dad's voice floated down from the top of the stairs. "Miki's not feeling well. I'll be down in a bit."

"Okay," I said. "Anything I can do? For Miki, I mean. Tea, juice…"

"Nope. I'm making risotto for dinner, so you could heat up some chicken stock if you like."

I went back into the kitchen and rooted around in the cupboards until I found a box of chicken stock. As I poured it into a pot, my dad came downstairs with some dirty dishes and loaded them into the dishwasher. He gave me a quick one-armed hug, and I caught a whiff of his awful medicated dandruff shampoo and felt the rasp of his beard in my hair. My dad is scruffy, but my friends tell me he's cute. I really wouldn't know. He has beautiful hands that he keeps soft with frequent applications of Jergens lotion (with aloe). He buffs his nails while we watch TV. He has a manicure every few months and he always wants me to come along, but that's just too weird. Even though he wears gloves and a mask to handle the preemies, he always wants his hands to be soft. He sings to the babies, the same songs he sang to me when I was little. His repertoire is entirely composed of songs with the word baby in the title. The babies (and probably a lot of nurses and new mothers) love him. He's always getting thank-you cards signed with tiny handprints. *Thanks for everything. You're the best. Dan and Sandy Jones and baby Georgia.* Miki met him when he was cooing "Come on, baby, light my fire" to a crack-addicted preemie. For better or worse, it's their song. He hired a Samoan band, complete with ukuleles and falsettos and a lot of tattoos, to sing it at their wedding. That and "Born to Be Wild," which is so not Dad that even the band cracked up.

Dad plugged the kettle in and leaned against the marble countertop as he waited for the water to boil.

"So, Julia," he said. "I need to talk to you…" His voice trailed off as he turned and opened the refrigerator and pulled out a hunk of fresh gingerroot. Ginger risotto? I hoped not.

"About what?" I said. He was acting weirder than usual, which was saying something. Had someone spotted me at

London Drugs buying the home pregnancy test? Had the library blown the whistle on my Internet searches?

He peeled the ginger and sliced it into thin disks, which he then tossed into the teapot. The kettle clicked off and he poured the hot water over the ginger. The kitchen smelled momentarily like Hawaii.

"Well, Miki's not really sick. I mean, she is, but not, you know, *sick* sick." He scratched his stubble and a few flakes of skin floated to the floor. "The ginger tea is for the nausea. You know, the morning sickness, except it's more like morning, noon and night sickness." He poured some tea into a cup and looked at me with a combination of pride and fear. "Miki's almost three months pregnant. You're going to be a big sister. We waited to tell you until we were sure everything was going to be okay. Miki's not that young and there are risks when you're older and…"

The poor guy. He'd probably been freaking out about telling me. Since he seemed to have forgotten that I wasn't seven anymore, I frowned and pouted for a while before I put him out of his misery. Long enough for him to babble on about not wanting to replace me and how I'd always be his baby and how there was no way they expected me to babysit all the time. Which was good news because extended babysitting didn't fit into my plans at all. It was kind of strange—the idea of my dad with a new baby—but he spends his days with babies and so does Miki, so it made sense for them to have one of their own, although I hoped they'd forgo the masks and gloves when they brought the baby home.

"What took you so long?" I finally said, and Dad, I'm ashamed to say, burst into tears and grabbed me and hugged me and danced me around the kitchen, singing "Baby Love" like Diana Ross on steroids. When he finally stopped, I handed him a square of paper towel and said, as nonchalantly as possible, "So, ginger tea is good for nausea?"

If he thought it was an odd question, he didn't say so. He just nodded and grinned idiotically and ran upstairs and dragged Miki out of bed and down to the kitchen. I have to say—she looked like shit on a stick. Way worse than Ruth. Miki's usual style is what Nana calls "tucked." She dresses in crisp white shirts and tailored suits—very expensive shirts and suits. She wears funky Fluevog shoes, multiple silver bangles and Venetian glass bead necklaces. Her black hair is short and spiky—sort of like the rest of her; her lips are full and red, her eyelashes thick and black, her skin white and unlined. Snow White with a stethoscope. Her bedside manner is as brisk as my father's is mellow, but she has her share of fans. On this day her hair was matted and sticking to her head, and she was wearing fuzzy pink slippers, old yoga pants and my dad's ancient gray UBC sweatshirt. Her face was the color of a pistachio and her lips were chapped.

Sarah N. Harvey

"Hey, Julia," she said. "I take it he told you."

"It's great, Miki," I said, wondering if a hug was in order and then deciding against it. Why start now? "Congratulations."

"Thanks," she mumbled as she took the cup of tea from my dad and lowered herself into a chair at the table. "Sorry to be so…lame. It's just that I wasn't ready for this." She bent her head over her teacup, but not before I saw a tear trickle down her pale cheek. Now that was something I hadn't seen before. "I've tried everything—ten meals a day, crackers at midnight, gallons of ginger tea. Nothing works. What if I'm one of those women who are nauseated for their entire pregnancy?" She looked up at my dad, who sat down beside her and took her hands in his.

"Maria said that was really rare, didn't she?"

"Yeah," Miki said. "Rare but not unheard of."

"Who's Maria?" I asked. All the nausea talk was starting to make me feel ill.

"Our midwife," Miki said. "We're having the baby at home."

"If we can," added my dad.

Miki shot him a look over her mug that gave me a pretty good idea of where their baby was going to be born.

"Barring major complications," Miki continued, "we're having a home birth. Maria is the best midwife in town, and I'm healthy and strong and well-informed. It shouldn't be a problem. I hate hospitals. We'll set everything up in the guest room—and, hey, I've got the best neonatal nurse and doctor around." She smiled at my dad, and I could see that she hadn't brushed her teeth for a while. There was a poppy seed stuck between her front teeth.

And since when did Miki hate hospitals? She practically lived on the wards, making life and death decisions on a daily basis and scaring the crap out of most of the staff. I thought she would love the idea of having her baby in a sterile environment where she could order people around, but apparently I'd misjudged her. She wanted to order people around in the comfort of her own home.

"When's the baby due?" I asked.

"Mid-June," my dad said.

"June fifteenth, to be exact," Miki said. If the baby knew what was good for it, it would arrive on schedule. Might as well start out on the right foot—punctuality is a big deal with Miki. Which is odd, since most of her little patients arrive really early.

I did some quick calculations in my head; Miki's baby was due six weeks before Ruth's, which could be useful. I sat down at the table and my dad offered me a mug of ginger tea. Out of solidarity, I tried some. It wasn't as bad as I expected, especially after I stirred in a couple of spoonfuls of honey, and I made a mental note to buy some gingerroot for Ruth. And some crackers.

"So, do you think I could interview Maria for a school project I'm doing on modern women in the workforce?" I asked. "I really want to talk to someone with a kind of alternative job. Everybody else is doing, like, bankers or lawyers. A midwife would be really cool." I wasn't exactly lying. I really did have to do a report for Social Studies. It wasn't exactly on women in the workforce—more like on why women shouldn't be in the workforce—but Miki and Dad didn't need to know that. With any luck, they'd put me in touch with this Maria person, and she could give me the lowdown on home birth. Maybe I could even convince Miki and Dad to let me assist at the delivery—although, to be honest, the idea kind of creeped me out.

"You can ask her yourself," Miki said. "She's coming over in about half an hour to give me a checkup. You can hang around if you like." Miki got up and headed upstairs. "Call me when she gets here—or better yet, talk to her first and then call me. I'm gonna go lie down—I feel like crap."

Dad rushed to help her back to bed, and I sat at the table, drinking ginger tea and formulating questions to ask Maria. By the time the doorbell rang, I had only thought of a few questions, but with any luck, Maria would be a talker. When I answered the door, the woman standing on the doorstep smiled and said, "Hi, Julia."

I blinked. I'd heard stories about midwives—how they were all old Birkenstock-wearing hippies who made groovy placenta stews after the babies were born and hadn't seen the inside of a hair salon since 1965. The woman standing on the front porch couldn't possibly be a midwife. For one thing, she was wearing stilettos; for another, she was Mark Grange's mother.

"Can I come in?" she said. "This bag's kinda heavy." She had a big red leather bag slung over one shoulder, and she carried a Starbucks travel mug in one hand and a cell phone in the other. Her fingernails matched her bag.

"Sure, Mrs. Grange," I mumbled as I stepped aside. Her stilettos clicked over the tile as she made her way to the kitchen. She looked at the pot of ginger tea and sniffed.

"She's still nauseous, huh?"

"Yeah," I said. "It's pretty bad." I hesitated. "Um, Mrs. Grange…"

"Please, call me Maria—my last name isn't Grange anyway. It's Ramirez."

"Oh," I said. "Sorry." She put her coffee and her phone on the table, kicked off her shoes and hefted the big bag onto a kitchen chair. Her feet were bare and her toenails were painted squid-ink blue. Ruth would approve. She hauled a coil-bound notebook, a blood-pressure cuff and a thing that looked like a walkie-talkie out of the bag and then took a sip of her drink.

"I'm always telling my clients to drink ginger tea but the stuff makes me gag." She waved the travel mug at me.

"Full-fat, mondo caffeine, that's me. Don't tell Miki. She thinks this is chamomile tea." She laughed and I could see the resemblance to Mark—wide smile, great teeth, dark curls, wicked gleam in big brown eyes.

"Um, Miki said it was okay for me to ask you a few questions before you do your checkup. She's really tired, and I've got this report for school..."

"Sure," she said. "What do you need to know?"

Five

"Christmas won't be Christmas without any presents,"
grumbled Jo, lying on the rug.

—Louisa May Alcott, *Little Women*

I don't remember how old I was when I first read *Little Women*, but I do remember that for years I begged my mother for a little sister. I conveniently disregarded the fact that she wasn't married, had no boyfriend, had never expressed a desire for another child and could not guarantee me a sister even if she wanted to. But I longed to be part of a big, warm, loving, noisy clan of females. I ended up with Ruth—the one-girl clan—and my own version of Jo's castles in the air. I even called my mother Marmee for a while, and I identified with all the sisters except Beth, the sappy one who dies. I still think of myself as a composite of the other three: ultra-responsible, kind Meg; selfish, spoiled Amy; smart tomboy Jo. Although I draw the line at ending up with a middle-aged German husband. I gave up on the little sister thing a long time ago, but Ruth and I still build castles in the air. For years our castle has been a really funky (in a good way) two-bedroom apartment in a city far away. We work at fabulous, high-paying jobs and have fabulous, highly paid boyfriends who take us on fabulously expensive vacations and don't expect us to cook, commit or clean toilets. The details are vague and variable—sometimes we live in LA and work in the film industry; sometimes we live in New York and work in the fashion industry; sometimes we live in London and work in publishing—but Ruth always works in marketing, and I'm always writing, and we always have a red leather couch. We remain inseparable and childless. Well, at least we got one thing right.

I LEARNED A lot from Maria the day I discovered that I was finally going to be a sister. A lot that I didn't need to know—like how long a midwife has to train and why some women give birth under water—and a lot that I did—like the importance of good nutrition and regular checkups. Lucky for me, Maria liked to talk and Miki stayed upstairs for a long time. When she finally did come down, I got to stay in the room while Maria examined her, which wasn't as weird as it sounds, since it didn't involve as much nudity as a day at the beach. Maria got me to record Miki's weight and blood pressure in the spiral notebook. Then she got out the walkie-talkie thing—she called it a Doppler—and we took turns listening to the baby's heartbeat, which was pretty amazing. I could hardly wait to tell Ruth. Miki gave me a little lecture about how much better Dopplers were than old-school fetoscopes, which couldn't pick up a heartbeat until around twenty weeks. If there was anything wrong with the baby, you knew so much sooner, which I guess is supposed to be a good thing. She seemed really happy that I was taking an interest, and I felt pretty bad that what she interpreted as interest was really just research. I mean, yeah, I was going to have a baby brother or sister, which was pretty cool—but I knew they didn't really need my help. And Ruth did. Miki and Dad had Maria, and each other and all the money and medical help they needed. Ruth had me. And I needed all the help I could get. I also needed a regular stethoscope (for listening to Ruth's heart), a Doppler and a blood-pressure cuff, at the very least. I had no idea how I was going to get them, but I knew I'd figure it out.

When she was packing all her stuff up, Maria said, "Marco used to come and help me with my ladies—when I couldn't afford a sitter. His job was to write the weights in the book. Just like you did today." She reached out and patted my hand. "Don't look so shocked. My ladies loved him— lots of kids are at home births, watching their little brothers and sisters be born—so they didn't mind Marco at all.

He was such a sweet little guy. It's been a long time since he came out with me. Too long."

A sweet little guy. Mark Grange. Hard to imagine. The kid has a mouth on him like Tony Soprano on a bad day. His mother was pretty amazing, though. You could tell that Miki felt better just being around her. More relaxed. In control, but not in a bad way. They talked about due dates and shoe sales and vitamins and when Miki should stop working. Before Maria left she gave me her business card. On the back she had written the name of a book that she said would be good for my research. "Call me anytime," she said. "Either of you. Anytime at all. My cell's always on."

WHEN I GOT to school on Monday, Ruth was back at her desk, looking, if anything, thinner and paler than she had on Saturday. Maybe the pregnancy glow came later. So far neither Miki or Ruth showed any signs of phosphorescence or incandescence or whatever.

"Glad to see you, Ruth," said Mrs. Gregory. "Feeling better?"

Ruth nodded and muttered, "Stomach flu sucks." She glared at me as if I was somehow responsible for making her lie to a teacher. Ruth has been lying to teachers since the first day of kindergarten, when she told Miss Fredericks that both Jesus *and* the Virgin Mary had appeared to her in a grape popsicle. Mrs. Gregory had written the morning meditation on the board. It said: *Ultimately, the problems and difficulties of life are all spiritual.* We had two minutes to think about it and eight minutes to discuss it. Ruth leaned over and whispered, "Yeah, like getting drunk and knocked up is a spiritual problem."

"Ruth," said Mrs. Gregory, "please meditate silently for a few moments and then share your thoughts with us."

We sat in silence for a minute or so, and then Ruth jumped to her feet, put her hand over her mouth and ran out of the room.

I stood up to follow her. "I'll go make sure she's okay. Maybe take her to the office."

There are distinct advantages to cultivating an aura of responsibility. Mrs. Gregory just smiled at me and nodded and said, "Ruth is very lucky to have you for a friend, Julia." She didn't know the half of it.

As I left the room, I could hear Rachel Greaves, who is a giant suckhole, saying that, like, war and world hunger were, like, spiritual problems because, like, if everyone just, like, followed Jesus it would all be, like, okay. It's just as well I had to leave the room. I wondered if she'd, like, think a punch in the nose was a, like, spiritual problem.

As I ran down the hall to the girls' washroom, Mr. Dooley's prayer for the safety of all those participating in the live nativity scene came over the PA. Last year the projectiles hurled from passing cars had been many and varied: a half-eaten Big Mac, a filthy SpongeBob SquarePants that landed on the Baby Jesus, and that old favorite, a flaming bag of shit.

I found Ruth staring into the mirror over one of the sinks. Not putting on lip-gloss or repairing her mascara. Just staring.

"I can't do this," she said.

"You have to," I said. "We decided. And anyway, I found out a lot of stuff yesterday from Maria—stuff that'll help."

"Maria?"

"Yeah—she's Miki's midwife."

"You told a midwife about me?" Ruth turned away from the mirror and grabbed my arm. "I thought we weren't going to tell anyone. And what do you mean—Miki's midwife?"

"Calm down," I said, pulling my arm away. "I didn't tell anyone anything. Miki's pregnant, she's got a midwife and I asked her a few questions. That's all. I said I was doing a report for school."

"You're gonna be a big sister?" Ruth squealed. "That's awesome. Why didn't you tell me?" She gave me the kind of look that usually precedes something painful—like a head-lock or a really big hug. It could go either way. I was glad to have taken her mind off her nausea but not so glad to be about to pay the price.

"I just found out on Saturday—and Miki's really sick, just like you. Maria recommended ginger tea and saltine crackers, and I have to get a bunch of equipment and a note-book and…"

"Whoa…back it up, sister," said Ruth. "You mean there's no, like, drug for this kinda shit? I hafta drink some fucking hippie tea and eat some lame crackers?"

"It can't hurt to try, can it?" I said.

THE NEXT DAY she nibbled on a cracker and the day after that she sipped the tea that I brought in a Tim Hortons travel mug.

"Tastes like piss," she said. "Hippie piss."

But she drank it, and her desk was a mess of cracker crumbs. I knew she was feeling better because she rolled her eyes and snorted when I told her that I was working on a special prenatal diet and exercise regime for her.

"Regime, huh? Sounds military. Right up your alley." Ruth saluted me as she swept the cracker crumbs onto the floor.

"At ease, recruit," I said. Ruth giggled and snapped a hair elastic at my head.

"So here's the deal," I continued. "You want to gain as little weight as possible and still have a healthy baby, right?"

Ruth yawned and said, "I guess."

"So you have to eat right and exercise regularly."

She groaned. "How am I gonna do that without anyone noticing? I mean, everyone knows I never exercise, and I never eat healthy food. I thought the whole idea was to, like, act normal."

"Well, yeah, that's the tricky part," I admitted. "But what if I do it too? The whole diet and exercise thing, I mean. It just doesn't seem fair to make you suffer alone. But when you think about it, who's really going to notice? Your parents? You don't eat with them anyway—not since Jonah left. And we'll still go to Mickey D's or DQ once in a while, just to keep up appearances—we just won't eat what we buy. We'll give it away to one of those guys who's always asking for spare change. Boost the karma quotient a bit. I'll tell my mom that you're going on a diet and I'm trying to be supportive. She'll love that. We'll go to the gym and stuff. No one will care. Trust me."

"Yeah, right, "Ruth said as she scraped some black nail polish off her thumbnail. "I get fat and have a baby and you get skinny. Sounds fair. Wish I'd thought of that."

She was right—the whole thing sounded insane and more than a little unfair. But what else could we do? And besides, I didn't want to be chubby, smart, reliable Julia anymore. I wanted to be a slimmer, hotter version of smart, reliable Julia. When Mark Grange had asked me when the baby was due, I'd laughed—not because it was funny, but because I didn't want him to see how much it hurt. It hurt the same way it did when I was little and I was playing in Ruth's backyard kiddie pool with Ruth's brother. Ruth's mother had a bunch of her church lady friends over and she pointed at me and said, "Oh look—it's Jonah and the whale." I couldn't help it that Ruth was pregnant, and I would help her any way I could, but if I lost a few pounds in the process, what was wrong with that?

EVERY YEAR IN the week before Christmas vacation started, Westland High did a ton of fundraising for one Christian charity or another. This year it was something to do with getting new computers for the school library and giving the old ones to a shelter downtown, which in my opinion was just a justification for spending a shitload of money on LCD screens and ergonomic keyboards and wireless Internet technology. I mean, all our online activity at school is monitored, lest we download porn or go into dubious chat rooms, so what's the point? Anyway, there was the live nativity pageant, a carol concert, a cookie exchange and the annual teachers vs. students basketball game. The teachers were heavily favored to win this year due to their new coach, Brandy's stepdad, a seven-foot-tall ex-college basketball coach from Georgia. Brandy's mom met him on a Christian Internet dating site, and he moved here a few months ago. He's a cool guy.

I've thought of asking him if he has any friends back in Georgia who'd like to date my mom, but I'm not sure she's ready for a giant black boyfriend. Stewart and Marshall had tried to get permission to put on a casino-night fundraiser—they called it Betting on Jesus—but it was, as they say, no dice. Also no roulette, no poker and definitely no blackjack. They had to be content with taking bets on the game, and they did a booming business in the second-floor boys' washroom, third stall from the left.

Any other year, Ruth would have been heckling Joseph and Mary, belting out lewd lyrics to the carols and running up and down the basketball court, pretending to be a Laker girl. This year she skipped the carol concert and confined her cheerleading activities to the occasional rude chant. She was kicked out after yelling,

You might be good at teaching
You might be good in class
But when it comes to basketball
We're gonna kick your ass.

Which turned out not to be true. All the cheering in the world couldn't help the Westland Warriors; the teachers beat them 92–74. High fives and Praise the Lords all round on the teacher's bench, with a few butt slaps for Coach Baylor. The Warriors muttered a lot about unfair coaching advantages. They didn't seem to remember what Our Lord said about turning the other cheek. At least not the kind

He was talking about. Apparently there was an unfortunate incident after the game at the live nativity scene—numerous young male cheeks were turned, and Mary almost had a coronary. The Three Wise Men took off after the offenders but were severely hampered by their long robes and the gifts they bore. The Warriors pulled up their shorts and scampered into Passmore Park, where they were later picked up for public drunkenness. Among those arrested was none other than Rick Greenway. One of Pastor Pete's parishioners, who works at the police station, told us that when he asked Mary if she could pick the offenders out of a lineup, she said she'd never seen their faces, but she'd be able to recognize one of them by the distinctive pimples on his butt. She said they reminded her of the Big Dipper. I guess when you're out in the cold holding a plastic Jesus while people drive by and throw things at you, you have a lot of time to look at the stars.

I told my mom that I had done some serious praying, and I felt that Our Savior wanted me to spend the next few months purifying my body and abstaining from all unhealthy habits. And when I was finished purifying and abstaining, He wanted me to go on a spiritual retreat. What God-fearing mother wouldn't want to hear that from her seventeen-year-old daughter? My mom nodded and continued working on a cross-stitched sampler pillow, which said, appropriately, *Come unto me all ye that are heavy laden.*

Sarah N. Harvey

I told my dad and Miki that I wanted to lose some weight, but they were so far gone into baby-land that they just nodded and smiled and asked me to go to the store for gelato. Apparently something called stracciatella gelato settled Miki's stomach. Unfortunately both its price and its calorie count made it off-limits for Ruth and me. Ruth didn't tell her parents anything—she never does. She has refused to eat with them since they sent Jonah away, so we put a cooler in her closet (she had sold her hope chest on eBay) and kept it stocked with healthy snacks. We cheated every now and again, and Ruth ate at my house a lot, under my mom's approving eye. We walked everywhere—to school, downtown, to the movies, to the store.

By Christmas Ruth's nausea was gone, and we had both lost five pounds. Such is the power of the no-junk-food diet. We decided to relax the food rules a bit for Christmas, although we swore we'd go easy on the mashed potatoes and gravy. I usually have three Christmas dinners: one restaurant dinner on Christmas Eve with my dad and Miki and Ruth, followed by gift-opening; one traditional turkey dinner with my mother and Nana on Christmas Day (after more gift-opening and church); and dinner on Boxing Day at Ruth's. Since Peggy claims to be too busy doing the Lord's work to cook, we eat food donated by Pastor Pete's loyal church ladies. Things like Mrs. Lowen's Pizza Casserole, Mrs. Marpenny's Bratwurst Soup and Mrs. Bingham's Mexican Lasagna.

64

I looked forward all year to Miss Chalfont's Texas-Missouri Beer Bread, although this year I ate only two pieces instead of my usual five. There are never any salads (unless you count tomato aspic, which isn't even food), and all vegetables are cooked beyond recognition. For dessert there was a gummy Sara Lee cheesecake. Ruth deigned to eat with her family, not because it was Christmas, but because Jonah was home for a week.

Seated at the table in Peggy's pristine dining room, the tacky nativity tree centerpiece lit up and playing "Silent Night," the table groaning under the weight of the casserole dishes, we held hands as Pastor Pete prayed for the heathens, the sinners, the homosexuals, the Jews, the members of Metallica and Slayer, anyone associated with hip-hop, and the makers of *Sex and the City*. It was a long prayer. Jonah was sitting next to me, holding my left hand in his right. As Pastor Pete detailed the Lord's plans to smite the evildoers at HBO, Jonah squeezed my hand. I turned my head slightly and opened my eyes long enough to see him wink at me before he bowed his head again. His hair had been buzzed off, military-style, but I remembered a particular dark damp curl that had caught on one of my rings. A few strands of his hair had come off in my hand. I have them still, in an envelope in my underwear drawer. I wondered what it would feel like to stroke his neck now. Fuzzy? Prickly? Cool? Pastor Pete's prayer finally came to an end, and I snatched my hand away from Jonah's before he could feel the sweat rising on my palm.

AFTER CHRISTMAS I began my research in earnest. Ruth and I walked to the library almost every day; she read magazines while I filled a notebook with information about fetal development, nutrition and the importance of maintaining a positive attitude. I thought I could cope with the physical stuff—I hoped I could anyway—but the attitude? That was another story. Even though I tried to interest Ruth in what I was learning, she wanted nothing to do with it. It was as if I was the one who was pregnant and she was the one along for the ride. Total role reversal. Her biggest concern seemed to be that she wasn't going to be able to show off her "bump," as she called it. There would be no clingy tank tops or skimpy dresses for Ruth. Just increasingly baggy T-shirts, exercise pants and sweatshirts. I would dress the same way, for solidarity purposes, but after the baby came I hoped to be shopping for something clingy and/or revealing myself. After all, I was going to be somebody's big sister—a role model, in fact. I had to look good.

Six

It was love at first sight.

—Joseph Heller, *Catch-22*

I'm not sure I believe in love at first sight. I mean, I first saw Jonah when I was five and he was seven, and Ruth was trying to bury him alive in the sandbox in their backyard. She was sitting on him, and he was howling, and his little snot-and-sand-encrusted face kept appearing out of the sand. I pulled Ruth off him and helped him up, and he ran into the house, screaming for his mother. Ruth was disgusted with me and kept on being disgusted with me over the years every time I defended Jonah against her. Maybe I have loved him from the beginning. Maybe it's not even love. *Catch-22* isn't about romantic love anyway. It's about war and what people will do to try to survive in combat. It's about defying authority in creative ways and about not getting killed in the process. It's about how wacky idealists like Ruth and born-again pragmatists like me are simultaneously brilliant and stupid. We were doing this insane thing—concealing Ruth's bump—and hoping not to get killed, metaphorically speaking. And we were caught in a classic Catch-22: We would be equally crazy whether we told anybody what was going on or not. We were engaged in a war in which our main weapon was our ability to lie convincingly. Usually I don't mind lying—I think of it as a legitimate creative exercise for a budding writer. But I hated lying to Jonah. Jonah is like the Texan in the army hospital in *Catch 22*: "good-natured, generous and likable." Unlike the Texan, who no one could stand after three days, Jonah just gets better with time.

We'd only had a couple of hours alone together over Christmas. My mom went out one evening, but she was gone long enough for me to determine that Jonah's buzz cut was as soft as the acrylic-pile snowsuit I had when I was six. Boot camp also had some unforeseen benefits—all that enforced exercise had given Jonah an impressive six-pack and the stamina of a triathlete. He was still Jonah, though—smart, funny, thoughtful (he brought condoms but put them away when I said I wasn't ready yet).

"I got accepted to chef school in Vancouver, Julia," he told me as we snuggled under my duvet and listened to *Kind of Blue*. I don't really like Miles Davis, but I can tolerate him under certain circumstances. "I got a full scholarship.

No one else knows. I start in September. I'll be there two years and then, who knows—LA, maybe, or New York or London."

I had a sudden vision of Jonah in the funky two-bedroom apartment that Ruth and I dreamed of—his hair grown out, exhausted and exhilarated from a night in a hellishly hot kitchen. In my vision I had opened a bottle of red wine and was sitting on his lap while Ruth regaled us with tales about her latest movie promotion. Copies of my new novel were on the bookshelf...

It didn't surprise me at all that Jonah had his own grand plan or that he had already put it in motion. It did surprise me that I felt so forlorn. It wasn't like I was his girlfriend or anything.

"That's awesome," I said, smoothing out the duvet while I struggled to control the quaver in my voice. "When will you tell your parents?"

He shrugged and rolled over onto his back, lacing his hands behind his head; his armpit hair was damp and curly and smelled faintly of stale deodorant. I ran my fingertips over his nose, lingering on the bump. Jonah's nose had been broken a few times: once by Ruth (with a Tonka truck), once when he tried (unsuccessfully) to do a skateboard trick called a Bomb Drop and once when he plowed into a tree in his parents' car. His nose is beautiful. As are his lips, which are both full (bottom) and chiseled (top). He smiles a lot, even though his teeth are crooked. There is also a small scar on his chin from when he fell into a rosebush when he was a toddler. I have memorized Jonah's face like a poem.

I desperately wanted to tell him about the baby, but Ruth would have killed me, and what good would it have done anyway? Maybe I'd be able to tell him in May when he came back from boot camp. Maybe not.

"So what's up with you and Ruthie?" he said. "You guys okay?"

You have no idea, I thought as I sat up and pulled on my T-shirt. He put his hand on my back, and I wondered if he could feel my heart accelerate.

"No big plans," I lied. "Just, you know, get through high school, leave home, that kinda thing."

"Cool," he said, running his hand up and down my spine as Miles went off on one of his interminable jangly riffs. "Ruthie seems a bit down, that's all. Sort of quiet— for her anyway. I just wanted to make sure she's okay. She looks great, though. Healthier. So do you." He sat up in bed, and I kept my back turned to him as he wrapped his arms around my waist and nestled his chin into my neck. "You look…" He paused and I wondered if he'd been about to say "thinner" and then thought better of it. Telling a girl she looks thinner is pretty much the same thing as saying, "You used to be a fat cow." Instead he said, "I notice you guys don't eat so much crap anymore."

I wanted to blurt it all out right then. I wanted to, but I didn't. I kept my face turned away from his and I kept lying. "Ruth's fine. There was this guy—he dumped her and it kinda hit her hard. She really liked him. But she's okay now."

"Who was he? Anyone I know?"

"He was nobody. Just some cretin on the basketball team." Shut up, Julia, shut up, I told myself.

"I could kick his ass if you like," he said. "Give him a good ol' Bible-thumpin' beat-down."

I laughed. "If anyone kicks his ass it'll be Ruth. But thanks for the offer."

"Keep me posted," Jonah said as he pulled on his jeans. "I worry about you guys."

"You don't need to—really," I said. "We're totally fine."

AS I HAD predicted, nobody paid the slightest bit of attention to our new healthy habits. After all, it was January—season of short-lived New Year's resolutions. Maybe when we're in therapy years from now, Ruth and I will say we wish our families had figured it out. At the moment, though, my parents' trust, Ruth's parents' general cluelessness and the self-absorption of our peers were distinct blessings.

"When am I gonna feel it kick?" Ruth asked as we walked home from school in late January.

"Movement is usually detectable from about sixteen weeks on," I said, parroting one of the books I had been reading.

"When's that, Einstein?"

"Another month or so—maybe a bit sooner." We'd been over this stuff so many times: her due date (sometime in late July—I'd tried about five different methods of calculation and got a different date each time), her mood swings (scary), the size of her breasts (impressive, unlike mine, which were shrinking), but she didn't seem to retain anything but water. And not even much of that yet. It was one of the things I checked every week, along with her blood pressure, her weight and her emotional state. I also measured her stomach, which she hated, even though it wasn't any bigger yet. I had managed to find a fetoscope and a blood-pressure cuff on eBay. I had to ask my mother if I could use her credit card to order Ruth a birthday present online, but even when she said yes, a Doppler was still out of the question. A $500 charge on her VISA would set off all her maternal alarm bells. I stole a tape measure from the sewing room at school, and I bought a really gorgeous lined journal and a special pen with purple ink to record all the information.

"Remember? I told you we'd be able to hear the heartbeat at around twenty weeks? You'll probably feel the baby kicking before that," I said. "It's so cool. I heard Miki's baby's heartbeat on the Doppler when she was only eleven weeks along, but fetoscopes aren't that sensitive. Wait till you hear it—it sounds like a tiny galloping horse."

"So you're saying I've got My Little Pony racing around in there," Ruth said with a grimace. "I always hated their stupid manes and those lame little brushes. I think of it more as a Smurf anyway. Probably Sassette. She was always my favorite. Smurfette was such a turd."

I had a sudden vision of Ruth popping out a little blue baby with red pigtails and pink overalls. Blue babies are not good. Blue babies mean a trip to the hospital. Maybe I needed to stop reading about all the possible complications of pregnancy and childbirth. I knew Ruth should be having blood tests and urine tests, that she might develop vaginal bleeding or gestational diabetes or have a breech baby. And what if she needed a caesarean or an episiotomy? I didn't want to think about it, but somebody had to. As we turned onto my street, Ruth was still babbling about how she had flushed Smurfette down the toilet when she was four. As I listened to her, my heart started racing, and I broke into a sweat. When we got to my house, she was still going on about the look on her dad's face when the plumber fished out not only Smurfette but also Pastor Pete's watch, Peggy's rhinestone cross and a handful of Jonah's Lego.

"Shut up," I yelled. I grabbed Ruth by the arm and swung her around to face me.

"What is your problem?" she screeched, swatting at my hand.

I grabbed her other arm and shook her. I didn't care if she punched me or slapped me or pushed me into the street. I just wanted her to stop talking.

"You're pregnant," I hissed. "You're not having a Smurf. Your baby is not a toy."

She glared at me, and two red spots appeared on her cheeks. "Don't you think I know that?" she said. "Don't you think I pay attention to all the shit you tell me—eat less, exercise more, try tofu, meditate, take my vitamins, do yoga? Don't you get that I still can't believe this is happening to me? That I don't want to believe it?" Tears formed in her eyes and she let them fall. "I'm scared, Julia. Fucking terrified. I'm not stupid—I know lots of things can go wrong. I just don't want to think about them. Not yet anyway. You can worry for both of us right now. I've done everything you've told me to do so far, haven't I?"

I nodded and moved my hands off her arms and up to her face. I felt bad for yelling at her, but I was scared too, and I had no one to talk to. No one at all.

"Your mascara's running. You look like Alice Cooper," I said as I stroked her cheeks. "C'mon. Let's go nuts and have some dip with our carrot sticks."

SEABISCUIT—WHICH IS what I called Miki and Dad's baby—was kicking up a storm by early February. Every weekend I laid my hands on her belly and we giggled when the baby's tiny elbows or heels pressed back. It felt like fetal tai chi. The bigger Miki's belly got, the mellower she became, as if the baby were a giant hit of long-acting weed. Everything about her was softer—her hair, her voice, her skin. The baby had sanded away all her sharp edges. I could hardly wait for Ruth to soften up too. Miki and Dad talked and sang to the baby all the time, so I did too. The books all said that babies can hear and respond to voices and music, so I wanted to make sure mine was one of those voices.

"Hey, little buddy," I said in the general direction of Miki's navel. "It's me, Julia, your big sister. We're all really anxious to meet you, but don't try and get out of there early. Enjoy it while you can—it's way more stressful on the outside. Trust me. Just chill out and don't give your parents a hard time."

Dad laughed. "What kid has ever listened to that advice?"

I pretended to look injured as I continued. "I'm going to sing you a special song now, and I'm going to sing it to you every week until you're born."

Miki groaned and said, "This better be good—and it better not have the word 'baby' in it."

"Trust me," I said. "It's not 'Maybe Baby' or 'Baby One

More Time' or even 'Baby Got Back,' although that one was tempting. You should learn it, Dad."

Miki groaned again, and I began to sing. "You are so beautiful…You are so beautiful…to me…"

By the time I got to the end, Dad and Miki had joined in and we were all in tears. That's how Maria found us—sobbing on the couch.

"I knocked but I guess you didn't hear me," she said. "The door was open. Is everything okay?"

We all nodded like dashboard dolls and grinned like fools. "Just singing to Seabiscuit," I said.

"Seabiscuit?" said Maria. "You're naming the baby after a horse?" She squeezed herself in between Miki and me on the couch and kicked off her shoes. Her nail polish was bright green. "Oh well," she said, patting Miki's belly, "at least it's better than Pilot Inspektor."

We must have looked pretty blank because she added, "You know—Jason Lee's kid. And then there's Moxie CrimeFighter and Speck and Sistine. I keep a file of weird celebrity baby names. Seabiscuit's not so bad."

Miki hauled herself up off the couch and announced, "We are definitely not calling our baby Seabiscuit. Although I am considering Flicka if it's a girl. And what do you think of Granite?" She arched one unplucked eyebrow, and we all burst out laughing again as she headed to the kitchen to put the kettle on.

"How about Quartz—no—Obsidian for a boy?" said Dad. "Obsidian Stevens-Riley. Very manly."

"Or what about Manitoba or Yukon?" I suggested. "So patriotic." I wondered how Joseph Heller came up with all the incredible names in *Catch-22*: Milo Minderbinder, Yossarian, Aarfy, Chief White Halfoat and my favorite, Major Major. It must be like naming a dozen children at once.

Maria and I trailed after Miki, pelting her with names— Iota, Kumquat, Quince, Napoleon, Dandelion—but Dad disappeared, muttering something about needing to download a recipe. A few minutes later I heard him guffaw and start to sing, "I like big butts and I cannot lie"—Sir Mix-a-Lot had made another conquest.

SHE FIRST FELT the baby kick in early February. We were in homeroom, listening to Rachel Greaves explain how Jesus wanted us to remain celibate out of respect for the sad fact that He got crucified before He had a chance to get laid. Suddenly Ruth gasped and yelled, "Holy Mary Mother of God!" and clutched her stomach with a look of absolute terror on her face. My first thought was that she was having a contraction, and I fell to my knees beside her, clasped her hands in mine and shrieked, "Sweet Jesus, bless our sister Ruth as she is filled with your Holy Spirit, and forgive our sister Rachel for implying that Jesus was horny."

I'm not above using the Almighty to create a diversion. Rachel started to cry as our classmates snickered, and Mrs. Gregory told her to pray for God's forgiveness. If God was anything like most fathers, he'd probably be proud that someone thought his boy was a stud. Ruth pressed my palm to her belly. It felt like Sassette was kickboxing; I could feel the pummeling of tiny heels and knobby elbows, and I'm pretty sure there was some head-butting going on in there.

"I know, sweetie," Ruth whispered. "I'd like to put some hurtin' on Rachel too, but we can't go around hitting every idiot we meet." It took me a minute to realize that she wasn't talking to me and that we were in far more trouble than I could ever have imagined. If Ruth got attached to her baby, there was no telling what might happen.

ON VALENTINE'S DAY, I gave Ruth a cupcake covered in pink icing when she came over to my house for her weekly checkup. Before she bit into it she dragged her index finger through the icing and drew a heart with it on her belly. "Happy Valentine's Day, Sassette," she said before she scraped up the icing and licked it off her fingers.

I did all the usual things that day: weighed her; took her blood pressure; checked her ankles for swelling; asked her if she was constipated, in pain, depressed, anxious, stuffed up, light-headed, dizzy or bleeding from any orifice. When I had recorded all my figures and all her responses (minus the foul language) in my journal, I got out the fetoscope and said, "Let's see if My Little Pony's awake." I hadn't yet been able to hear the baby's heartbeat, but I figured it had to happen soon, and it would be an even better Valentine's Day present than a cupcake.

I bent over and placed the fetoscope on her belly, and suddenly there it was—the thunder of tiny hoofs. I must have gasped, because Ruth yanked the fetoscope out of my ears, jammed the earpieces into place, hunched over, held her breath and listened.

"Omigod, omigod, omigod," she whispered. Her face turned the color of a McIntosh apple, and she made a strange choking noise. I put my hand on her shoulder and she shrugged it off, her face rosy and rapt. After about five minutes, she handed the fetoscope back to me, straightened up, hugged me and mumbled, "Thank you."

"For what?"

"For looking after us."

"No problem," I said. And I meant it.

After that, Ruth was a much better patient. She listened to the baby every week with the same goofy expression on her face, and she grumbled a lot about the fact that I was losing weight while she was gaining, but she was surprisingly good-humored about all the changes to her body and mine.

She even joked that the best thing about being pregnant was getting out of PE with a forged note from Dr. Mishkin.

IN THE MONTHS that followed, every time I examined her I'd go over the plan again: "I told my mother I wanted to go on a spiritual retreat in late July, and she said I could go as long as I take you with me. She's arranged for us to use a cabin belonging to one of the women in her aerobics class. After the baby is born"—I always glossed over the actual birth—"we'll leave it in your dad's church right before a service. Someone will call Social Services and the baby will go to a good home. No one will ever know who the mother was. And then we'll finish school and take off, just the way we always said we would." Even as I talked about New York and LA and London, about our apartment and our jobs, I kept reminding myself that women give birth in weirder and more dangerous circumstances than these. In airplane bathrooms, in high school washrooms, in rice paddies, in prisons.

For a while Ruth continued to have whispered conversations with little Sassette, but as time went by and it became more and more difficult for her to conceal the pregnancy, she started to moan, "Get it out of me," more often. The day she realized she had stretch marks was a dark day indeed, and when her ankles started to swell she started to act like the whole thing was my fault. By the middle of June, when Miki and Dad's baby was born, I was the only one on speaking terms with the baby that Ruth now referred to as the Spawn of Satan.

Seven

In the great forest a little elephant is born.
—Jean de Brunhoff, *The Story of Babar*

Babar has everything you could possibly want in a story: it's short, it has really amazing pictures and it makes its point in less than fifty pages. It starts with a birth and ends with a marriage, which is a classic literary pattern, according to Mrs. Hopper. In between are tons of the things that make life worth living: exotic travel, shopping, cool clothes, great food, a gorgeous red car, good friends and a loving family. Not to mention true love, spiky golden crowns, poisonous mushrooms and a hot air balloon. It's also full of emotion: fear (what happens to Babar's mother still scares the crap out of me); gratitude (the Old Lady adopts Babar); pleasure (the Old Lady lets Babar do pretty much whatever he wants); sadness (he misses his mother and his jungle home); joy (his cousins turn up) and triumph (Babar marries his cousin

Celeste—apparently that's not incest if you're an elephant—and becomes King of the Elephants). I love it that the Old Lady knows exactly what Babar needs (an elegant green suit, a simple meal and a good night's sleep) and that they function as a family—a really weird family, but what other kind is there? Is there any such thing as a normal family? Maybe it's true, what Tolstoy says in the first line of *Anna Karenina*: "Happy families are all alike; every unhappy family is unhappy in its own way." Which is a great opening line, for sure, but since I still haven't waded through the book, I don't know how he goes about proving his theory. It makes happy families sound boring and undesirable, but I learned from *Babar* that there's nothing dull about a happy family.

For instance: Miki and Dad are really happy. After she stopped being nauseous and started to enjoy food again, Miki decided that a bit of weight gain wasn't such a bad thing. "Baby Got Back" became her theme song, and she danced around the house shaking her ass and singing, "So Cosmo says you're fat, well I ain't down with that." Not dull. The sight of my dad practicing to be Miki's labor coach wasn't dull either (he looked like a demented frog when he practiced the breathing exercises), and his sudden interest in decorating the baby's room was equally bizarre. He tried out various themes—rainbows, flamingos, teddy bears, suns and moons, tropical fish, jungle beasts—but he couldn't settle on one. He chose colors and then painted them out.

He put up and stripped off five different wallpaper friezes and hung about ten different mobiles before Miki called a halt to the madness by threatening to ask her mother, Irina, to come for an interior design consultation.

Miki's mother is terrifying. She makes Miki (even the pre-pregnancy, skinny-ass, uptight Miki) seem like a total slob. Fortunately Irina lives in the United Arab Emirates or somewhere like that, where she designs gold bathrooms for rich Arab dudes. Irina is about as far from dull as you can get, but not in a good way. My dad can't stand her. After Miki threatened him, he painted the baby's room a buttery yellow with glossy white trim, put up a Winnie-the-Pooh frieze and hung a farmyard animal mobile that played "The Farmer in the Dell." Miki was happy. Dad was happy. So happy that they asked me if I wanted to attend the birth. Now, you have to admit, that's not dull.

In mid-June, the Beach Boys' "Don't Worry, Baby" woke me up in the middle of the night. It was the ringtone I'd set to alert me that Dad was calling (the ringtone I set for my mom is "What's the Buzz" from *Jesus Christ Superstar*), but I didn't recognize the voice on the phone.

"Julia, wake up."

"Unh." I wiped the drool from my chin.

"Wake up, Julia."

"Who is this?" I sat up in bed and checked the time and the call display: 2:00 AM and Dad's number, but definitely not Dad.

"Julia." The voice started to sound a bit impatient and slightly familiar now that I was waking up. "Wake up and get dressed. The baby's coming and they want you here."

"Maria?" I said. "The baby's coming? Now?" As if babies only arrived in the daytime. I knew better.

She laughed. "Yeah, now. Everything's fine, but I gotta run. Miki needs me. Your dad is—how can I say it—?"

"Useless?" I offered.

"Not useless, exactly." Maria giggled. "Just...*ansioso*...in a dither. So grab a cab and get your butt over here. It'll be fun."

She hung up, and I pulled on my sweats and wrote a note to my mom. When I'd told her I was going to be attending the birth, she looked as if I'd punched her in the gut, but all she said was, "Don't you find that...odd?" I didn't want to upset her again, but she woke up as I tiptoed through the living room.

"Go back to sleep, Mom. Miki's in labor. I'm heading over there."

"What?" she mumbled. "Where?"

"I'm going to Dad's. Go back to sleep. I'll call you later."

"How are you getting there?"

"I'll call a cab—it's okay."

She sat up on the sofabed and reached for her robe. "I'll drive you." She slid her feet into her fluffy blue slippers, grabbed her purse and headed for the door.

"You're going like that?" I said. My mother never leaves the house looking anything but "put together" as Nana calls it. Never. She even wears makeup to her aerobics class, and I swear she irons her T-shirts.

"You want a ride or not?" she said as she fished her keys out of her bag. "It's not like I'm getting out of the car, for heaven's sake. It's two o'clock in the morning."

I followed her out to the elevator and we rode down to the parking garage in silence. As soon as we got in the car, she turned on the radio. I didn't try to talk until we got close to Dad's. For once I found the Christian soft rock soothing. Reassuring even.

"Mom?"

"Uh-huh."

"Thanks for doing this."

"It's okay. I don't like you out alone at night."

"I know it's hard for you…" I began, but she reached over and patted my knee.

"Don't, Julia. It's okay."

I could see this was going nowhere, but I really wished she'd say something—anything—about what she was feeling. She seemed calm, but she was always calm. She was calm when I broke my ankle falling off the monkey bars in grade three. She was calm when I had a temperature of 107 degrees and told her that Michael Jackson was dancing on my bed. She was calm when Ruth and I used her crystal wineglasses at our lemonade stand. But this was different. Her ex-husband's new wife was having a baby. I was going to have a baby brother or sister. Was she angry? Sad? Resigned? Bitter? Envious? Or maybe she was just tired. Tired of being a single parent. Tired of worrying about money. Tired of her job. I knew there was no point asking—especially not at two in the morning on the way to Dad's house.

When we got there, I gave her a quick hug and a kiss on the cheek.

"I'll call you tomorrow—I mean today. When it's over."

She nodded. "Take care, Julia," she said and as I shut the door she added, "Tell your dad I'm praying for Miki and the baby."

I stood in the driveway as she backed out. Praying for Miki and the baby. But not for my dad. It was better than nothing.

When I got inside, the first thing I heard was Miki screaming "Sonofabitch" at the top of her lungs. I don't remember reading about that being part of the labor routine, but then again, I didn't go to the classes. I did remember something about the dreaded "transition stage" of labor, when women typically tell whoever got them pregnant to fuck off and die. I was really looking forward to Ruth's transition. I'd be lucky to escape without needing medical attention myself.

I went upstairs to the birthing room, aka the guest bedroom, which had been tastefully outfitted with rubber sheets, piles of fluffy white towels and a table covered in a white cloth. On the table were the tools of Maria's trade: Doppler, stethoscope, blood-pressure cuff, rubber gloves, plastic clamps for the umbilical cord, teensy bulb syringes, cotton balls, a tiny little white toque, some flannel blankets and a whole lot of other stuff I knew I'd never be able to get my hands on. Unless, of course, some of it made its way into my backpack while Miki was in labor. I just couldn't see ordering that kind of stuff on eBay. There was an oxygen tank tucked away in the corner beside an IV pole. If Ruth needed either oxygen or an IV, we'd be on our way to the nearest hospital faster than beer turns into piss. Beside the IV pole was a camping cooler. I peeked inside and saw bottled water, lemonade, orange juice, ice packs and a bottle of champagne. Maria really covered all the bases.

The rest of the room was as un-clinical as possible. White candles flickered in wall sconces, and the scent of lavender and geranium—Miki's favorite aromatherapy combo—filled the room. The mom-to-be was sitting up in the bed wearing a pink T-shirt that said *Doctors Do It with Patience.* Dad was holding her hand while she yelled at him. Maria was barefoot and smiling, as usual. She introduced me to a midwife named Lisa, who would be monitoring the baby while Maria looked after Miki. Standard practice for a home birth, Maria said. Nothing to worry about. Bossa nova music played on the portable stereo. Imagine hearing "The Girl From

Ipanema" as you came into this world. You'd start life off feeling warm and relaxed and languorous. Just another day at the beach. Not for Miki, though, apparently.

"Hey, Julia," Dad said. "I'm glad you're here. It's going great."

"Maybe for you it is," Miki snarled. "Some of us are in agony. Some of us are taking a vow of celibacy. Some of us are wishing we'd never met you."

"I know, hon. Breathe with me, Miki." Dad started to puff and pant like the Little Engine That Could, and Miki punched him in the nose. Which proves my point about happy families not being dull. Move over, Mr. Tolstoy.

"I'll take over," Maria said, prying Miki's hand out of Dad's. "Take a break, Dan. Put some ice on your nose. There's ice packs in the cooler."

For a second I thought he was going to refuse, but then Miki yelled, "Go, motherfucker!" and he went. Maria motioned to me to sit on the other side of the bed.

"Do the breathing with her, Julia. We're getting close. It all went pretty fast—that's why we didn't call you earlier." Maria wiped Miki's face with a damp washcloth and murmured, "Little Seabiscuit's on his way. Not too long now. Hang in there."

Lisa put the Doppler on Miki's belly. "Baby sounds good, really good."

"*Fuerte*," said Maria. "Strong—like his mother."

Miki smiled at Maria and started to breathe with me. *Hee-hee-who. Hee-hee-who.* My dad stood at the end of the bed and did some massage thing on her feet. Amazingly, she didn't kick him.

"Time the contractions for me, Julia," Maria said, handing me a stopwatch. "I have to get ready."

Miki groaned and said, "I wanna push. Now!"

"Not yet, *mi querida*. Soon. Tell Julia when the next one starts."

I stared at the stopwatch and listened to Miki breathe. She squeezed my hand when a contraction started, and when I could move my hand again, I knew the contraction was over. After three contractions I was ready to tell her to push. Anything to get her to stop breaking the bones in my hand.

"Two minutes apart," I said. "Ninety seconds long."

"I have to push!"

"Soon, Miki," Maria said. She positioned herself between Miki's legs and motioned my dad down next to her. "Are you ready, Dan? 'Cause your baby is."

Dad nodded, and I continued to hold Miki's hand as she pushed the baby out and Dad caught it. I don't know how long it took—maybe ten minutes, maybe more—but by the end we were all crying (my hand hurt like crazy, but that was only one of the reasons I was crying) and laughing. Dad clamped and cut the cord, and then he put the baby—my little brother—on Miki's chest. He wasn't a pretty sight, but boy, did he have some lungs on him. And balls. He rooted around on Miki's breast, and Dad couldn't stop crying and kissing Miki's face and arms and neck. Maria finally gave him a job—massaging Miki's back—and pretty soon she delivered the placenta, which was, in my opinion, pretty gross. Thank God no one suggested making stew. My stomach hurt just looking at it.

People talk about the miracle of birth, but, strictly speaking, it's not miraculous. A miracle has something to do with divine intervention or is an event that's extremely unusual. And let's face it, giving birth is as common as dirt and, unless you're one of those freaks who believe that sex is a religious experience, there's nothing divine about any of it, which makes it pretty hard to explain why all of us—even Maria and Lisa, who'd seen it all before a zillion times—acted as if something greater than ourselves was present in the guest room. I have never felt closer to anybody than I did to Dad and Miki and the baby that night. Not to Jonah or Ruth or my mother. The candles, the scent of flowers, the music—it was like being in the perfect church, full of joy and laughter and the astonishing presence of a brand-new human being. For about five minutes I considered whether my mother might be right, that there really is a God and that He is good and worthy of praise. Then I looked at my baby brother and at the two people who created him, and I didn't want to give the credit to anyone but them. For loving each other enough to go through this whole messy business.

I helped Maria and Lisa with the post-birth routine— weighing, measuring, counting fingers and toes, cleaning the baby with soft cloths, putting on his teensy diaper, his wee sleeper and his tiny hat. When he was wrapped snugly in a flannel blanket ("swaddled" is such an ugly word), Maria handed him to Dad and then Dad passed him to me and said, "Julia, may I present your brother, Timothy Boone Stevens-Riley."

I took him in my arms—all seven pounds, seven ounces of him—and held him close to my chest. "Hey, little buddy," I crooned down at him. "Glad to meet you. I'm your big sister Julia. And no little brother of mine is going to be called Timmy, so I guess you're Boone."

I looked over at Miki and Dad, half expecting them to argue with me, but all they did was gaze at the baby and nod and smile. I liked them that way. It wouldn't last, so I was going to enjoy it while I could.

"We thought you might say that," Dad said. "Boone it is, then. When he's thirteen and he wants to change his name, he can take it up with you."

"Cool," I said as Boone's tiny mouth puckered and a little mew escaped his lips. One skinny, wrinkled, little-old-man hand escaped the blanket and wandered toward my face. I kissed his translucent fingers and wondered how Ruth was ever going to give up the Spawn of Satan. I wanted to hold Boone forever, and he wasn't even mine.

I MADE BREAKFAST for everybody the morning Boone was born: bacon, eggs, toast, hash browns, strong coffee, fresh-squeezed juice and blackberry jam. Miki was drowsy, but she devoured six slices of bacon before she nodded off. Boone lay on her chest making funky snuffling noises, and Dad sat on the edge of the bed and dripped jam on the blanket while he stared at his son. Lisa left to go home and sleep. Maria and I took our plates downstairs and ate at the kitchen table.

"You're good at this," she said between mouthfuls of egg. "Really good. Most kids are pretty squeamish at a birth. Hell, most adults can't handle it." She paused to take a swig of coffee. "It was nice having an extra pair of hands."

"You're welcome," I mumbled. "I'm glad I was there." And it was true. When they'd first asked me to attend the birth, I'd thought of it as research. Observe, take notes, ask questions, steal supplies. That kind of thing. I hadn't reckoned on participating or enjoying myself or feeling profoundly changed by the appearance of my baby brother.

"Miki was lucky," Maria said. "No complications, great support. I wish they were all like this." She put her feet up on a chair and sighed.

"They're not?" I asked, even though I knew they weren't.

"Are you kidding? First births especially—lots of surprises."

My anxiety must have showed on my face, because Maria reached over and patted my cheek.

"It's okay, Julia. It's all over. Miki's fine. The baby's beautiful and healthy. Your dad's over the moon. Don't worry."

I nodded and mumbled something about being tired—which was true. I'd never been so tired. Or so wired. I put my head down on the table and started to shake. Maria leaned over and stroked my hair away from my face.

"It's the adrenaline rush, sweetie. It's wearing off and it leaves you all jittery and feeling like you have to cry, right?"

I nodded into the place mat. Almost jittery enough to blurt out that Ruth was six weeks away from having her first child and that I was going to be her midwife. Almost jittery enough to grab Maria and confess that I'd stolen an amnihook and two cord clamps from her. Almost, but not quite.

Maria wrapped me in a fleece blanket, made me a cup of honey-sweetened herbal tea and said, "Stay warm, hon. Drink some tea. Get some sleep if you can. I'm going to check on Miki and Boone, and then I'll be on my way. I'll be back later today. Call me if you need me. Okay?"

"Okay," I muttered from my fleece cocoon. "Thanks. Later." I sat at the kitchen table for a long time. My heart finally slowed down, and I eventually stopped shaking. The house was quiet after Maria left. My brother was upstairs and everyone was fine. I wished I felt better. I couldn't stop thinking about what Maria had said about first births and surprises. Ruth was always surprising me—why would she stop now?

Eight

When shall we three meet again?
In thunder, lightning or in rain?
—William Shakespeare, *Macbeth*

Macbeth is my all-time favorite Shakespeare play. I still don't understand why my classmates don't love it too. Especially the guys, who can't seem to get past what Stewart calls "the fruity language" to the sheer goriness of it all. Guys who will shell out ten bucks to see Uma Thurman decapitate her enemies are completely baffled by *Macbeth*. Lady Macbeth alone is worth slogging through any number of soliloquies about Scottish politics. I love it that the most ruthlessly ambitious, bloodthirsty, cruel and manipulative person in the play is a woman. Not that I approve of her behavior, but, let's face it, she's kind of Donald Trump in drag, with better hair and none of the opportunities. Like The Donald's wives, the only way Lady M can get any power is through her husband, which is pretty sad in any century.

I wrote a paper about Lady Macbeth called "McMommie Dearest," which my English teacher didn't think was funny. She also didn't appreciate my views on women and ambition, even though I went to great lengths to point out that killing people is an extremely ill-advised and risky method of personal advancement, as Lady M discovered. Having a career and being financially independent is a much better approach and involves far less sleepwalking and hand-washing. For this, I got a C, which for me is almost a failing grade. The whole "not of woman born" thing is all about a brutal caesarean section, by the way, just in case you were thinking that "untimely ripp'd" meant having a six-pack at the age of seven. So it's no wonder that after I fell asleep at the kitchen table after Boone's birth, I dreamt that Lady Macbeth (who looked like Cruella de Vil) was delivering Ruth's baby by caesarean, assisted by three life-size Barbie dolls. Very scary. So much for sleep knitting up the "ravelled sleeve of care."

When I woke up I had grooves on my cheek from the ridges on the place mat, a headache the size of Montana and—wouldn't you know it—cramps. Which only confirmed that there really is no God, not a loving one anyway. A loving God wouldn't allow a teenage girl to get pregnant the first time she has sex. A loving God would make sure my mom, who prays to Him at least ten times a day, was as happy as my dad, who doesn't even believe He exists.

A loving God would not smite me with cramps five days early or make me solely responsible for the safe delivery of my best friend's baby.

SCHOOL WAS ALMOST over for the year, and I was beginning to wonder if my plan was going to work. So far, no one had paid much attention to Ruth's size—all they saw was a big girl getting a bit bigger—but that was part of the problem.

"I'm sick of hiding out at the library," Ruth complained soon after Boone was born. "I never thought I'd say this, but I miss going to school. I'm tired of making up lame excuses for being absent. I'm bored with signing my own notes. I'm missing all the cool end-of-year stuff. All the parties."

"It'll be over soon," I said as soothingly as possible. That was my mantra when she started to whine. We were in my room, and I was making lists of things I had to get to prepare for the birth—things like diapers and blankets and rubber sheets. My babysitting money was dwindling by the second. Ruth, as usual, was lying on my bed reading a magazine—a magazine, I might add, bought and paid for by me. "And here's a thought," I muttered. "Maybe you could help out a bit with the preparations."

"What did you say?" Ruth glared at me as if I had announced that I was going to sell tickets to the delivery. "You must be joking," she said. "In case you haven't noticed, I'm the one who's doing the important work—the gestating. Isn't that what you like to call it? I'm the one who's fat. I'm the one who can't go out in public. I'm the one who has to eat lean protein and celery sticks. I'm the one who has to wear ugly clothes. I'm the one who's going to have the contractions. And the leaky boobs and the post-baby fat."

By this time Ruth was screaming and, even worse, clutching my Minnie Mouse alarm clock. I ducked just as it flew over my head and slammed into the wall behind me. I'd had that clock since I was six and my mom and I went to Disneyland. I picked it up and put it on my desk. Amazingly, it was still ticking. Like a bomb. Very appropriate, since Ruth seemed to have exploded, and I was about to.

"And you," Ruth roared, "what are *you* doing? Getting skinnier by the second, talking to hot guys, oh, and yeah, I forgot—making your stupid lists. In the meantime, I can't sleep, my ass hurts, I've got heartburn and I have to pee all the time."

Suddenly all the lying, the dieting, the labor coaching just seemed pointless and meaningless and stupid. There wasn't any point in getting angry with her. We weren't going to get away with it. It was that simple. Hiding Ruth's pregnancy had become as difficult as concealing a giraffe in a swimming pool. On the rare occasions she was at school,

I diverted attention from her ever-expanding girth by wearing really skanky outfits. Who's going to look at the fat chick in the yoga pants and baggy sweatshirt when her friend is wearing stilettos and a denim micro-mini with a pink satin camisole from Victoria's Secret (via Miki's closet). I figured Miki wouldn't be needing it anytime soon—her boobs were about a forty-four triple D. And they leaked. All Boone had to do was sniffle and Miki turned into a fountain. Anyway, I was the decoy, and my outfits were strictly camouflage, but I could understand why it pissed Ruth off. I was getting a lot of attention from guys (most of it unwanted) and she was getting none. Five different guys had asked me out to five different end-of-the-year parties. Ruth loves being the center of attention; I don't. Well, not much, anyway. Yes, I highlighted my hair. Yes, I bought new clothes, but I thought she understood that I was still the same girl—kind, studious, thoughtful—just hotter. Obviously I was wrong. Maybe I was wrong about everything.

"You want to stop?" I asked.

"Stop?"

"Yeah—stop hiding it. Tell your folks. Have the baby in the hospital. Just—you know—stop."

"Are you nuts?" Ruth said, looking at me as if I had sprouted horns. "Why would I stop now?"

I took a deep breath and tried to remember everything I had read about the emotional state of women in late pregnancy. The words "irrational" and "fearful" came to mind, as did the word "hemorrhoids." You didn't have to be pregnant to be irrational and afraid. I knew because I was feeling a bit of both myself. But I was pretty sure I didn't have hemorrhoids, and that alone made my life better than Ruth's.

"I make lists because I'm nervous," I explained. "They help me calm down."

"You? Nervous?" Ruth said. "Why?"

I laughed and walked over to my bed and lay down beside her. "Oh, let me count the ways," I said.

"No, seriously," she said, "it's gonna be fine. I mean, you helped out when Boone was born, so you know what to do. And I've done everything you told me to do, and you've been reading books about childbirth for months now. It has to be okay. It just has to."

Ruth was lying on her back, and her belly looked like a small smooth continent rising from a blue duvet sea. How could we hope to hide it for five more weeks?

"The Karate Kid's at it again," Ruth said, grabbing my hand and placing it near her belly button. "She's getting in shape for her big entrance."

We lay there for a few minutes, giggling and watching Ruth's belly ripple and surge.

"It's weird, isn't it?" Ruth said.

"What?"

"That she's so close to us and so far away at the same time. We can almost see her and yet she's in her own little world."

"Yeah," I said. "It's weird, all right."

IN EARLY JULY I got a part-time job downtown at a chain bookstore. I needed the money and Ruth needed an excuse to be away from home. She told her parents she had a job at the bookstore too, and we'd go downtown together on the bus; Ruth would head to the library while I went to work. I made her a book list, but I'm pretty sure all she read were magazines. When my shift was over, we walked home. I'd fill Ruth in on what had happened at work and she'd report on the latest Hollywood scandal. She had to pee about every five minutes, but she seemed almost happy. She didn't even get mad when guys hit on me, mostly because I blew them off. Jonah was due home any day, and that cheered her up. It terrified me, but in a sort of great way, like when you're on the Ferris wheel and it stops at the top.

"You packed all that stuff I put on your list?" I asked one day when we were in the park having a picnic and watching all the moms with their little kids.

"Yup," she said. "Although I don't know why I need my bathing suit. It's not like I'm going to wear it."

I explained for the hundredth time that it had to look as if we were going on a vacation, bathing suits and all. The cabin we were going to was beside a lake. And who knew? Maybe Ruth would decide to have one of those underwater births. Or maybe she'd just want to go for a swim. Knowing her, she wouldn't bother with a suit.

"Your mom's driving us, right?" Ruth asked.

"Next Saturday—bright and early."

Ruth groaned. "What if the baby's late?"

"Then we call and say we've just had some sort of vision of Jesus in a bowl of Cheerios and we need to stay away longer. Talk to God some more. The cabin's free until Labor Day. No pun intended."

"Ha bloody ha," Ruth said. She ate another piece of chicken and gazed at a girl about our age pushing a baby in a stroller. "Do you think that's her kid?"

"I dunno," I said. "Could be, I guess. Why?"

"No reason."

THE NIGHT BEFORE we were supposed to go to the cabin, my mother came down with a wicked stomach flu. In the morning she was too weak to stand up, let alone drive for two hours.

"I'm sorry, honey," she said. "You'll have to ask Ruth's parents for a ride."

"They're leading a workshop this weekend. Something about mission statements for marriages."

My mom winced and clamped her hand over her mouth. I slid a plastic ice-cream bucket toward her, but she shook her head and motioned it away. "How about your dad?"

"Away," I said, sparing her the details of Dad and Miki's weekend trip with Boone to Tofino. Baby's first room service. I was starting to feel sick myself, and I prayed I hadn't caught whatever she had.

"Oh." She groaned. "Pass me the bucket."

I went to the kitchen and called Ruth. "My mom's really sick. We're going to have to wait a couple of days."

"No way." Ruth sounded adamant.

"Don't freak out. It'll be fine."

"Contractions," Ruth hissed.

"What?"

"Contractions," she hissed again. "I've been having contractions. And my mom's in the next room."

"They're probably just Braxton Hicks," I whispered. "You know—false labor. I told you about that."

"They're not Braxton Hicks. We have to go—now."

"There's no one to drive us."

"I'll ask Jonah. He came home last night. He was only here five minutes and he looked like he wanted to split. He'll drive us."

"You can't tell him, Ruth. Not a word."

"I'm not an idiot," said Ruth before she hung up. "We'll be there before lunch."

WHEN THEY CAME to pick me up a few hours later, the first thing Jonah said was, "Where's the thunder, lightning and rain?"

"It's July, asshole," said Ruth. "Not January."

"Julia knows what I mean, don't you, Julia?" Jonah said, giving me a quick hug and a kiss on the top of my head. He was wearing baggy red board shorts and a tight T-shirt that said *Miles, Monk, Trane.* I bet his parents loved that. It was all I could do not to grab his ass. I settled for landing a light kiss on his neck.

"'When shall we three meet again? In thunder, lightning or in rain?'" I recited.

"'When the hurlyburly's done, when the battle's lost and won,'" Jonah replied.

"Jesus Christ, you guys," said Ruth. "Get a room."

It was a whole new interpretation of *Macbeth,* which, trust me, isn't usually thought of as one of Shakespeare's more romantic plays. After Jonah and I stopped laughing, we crammed all my stuff into Pastor Pete's old Dodge Caravan and took off for the lake. I rode shotgun, since Ruth said she wanted to sleep in the back of the van. We listened to one of Jonah's Thelonious Monk CDs for a while and stopped at a Dairy Queen after we'd been on the road for about an hour.

"So, Mom says you guys are going on a retreat," Jonah said as we got back in the car with our hot fudge sundaes.

"Yup," I said, trying not to look at him. I couldn't help smelling him though, the familiar combination of sweat and deodorant and something sweet—cinnamon buns, maybe, or some kind of pie. I'd never figured out what it was. Just that it made me feel like a kitten with a catnip mouse.

"Or maybe you're just going to be partying at the lake," he continued. "Have a few friends over. Fire up the barbie. You sure brought enough stuff."

I snuck a look at him. Was he serious? His profile gave nothing away, although I noticed that he had a zit on his chin and looked as if he had cut himself shaving. I was happy about the zit; perfection is so hard to deal with.

"Nothing like that," I assured him. " Just taking a break. Swimming, hiking, hanging out. Just the two of us, right, Ruth?" Ruth grunted from the backseat.

"What did you say, little sis?"

"Nothing." Even to me, Ruth sounded odd. Breathless, as if she'd been running a marathon.

"You okay back there?" I asked. "If you're carsick, we can trade places." I was so anxious I felt like I was going to puke all over Pastor Pete's camo seat covers; in my head

I was pleading: Please, please, please Ruth, don't have the baby now. Not in the car, not with Jonah. Hold on just a bit longer. Cross your legs, Think good thoughts. Pray.

"I'm okay," Ruth mumbled. "I've got a, uh, charley horse. In my leg. I've been getting them every ten minutes, Julia. For, like, three hours. And I really need to pee."

"Every ten minutes?" I squeaked. "For three hours? Why didn't you tell me?"

As I turned around to talk to Ruth, I heard the click of the turn signal and felt the van move to the right and slow down. Jonah was pulling over. Oh, God, he was pulling over. He couldn't pull over. We had to get to the cabin—and fast.

"Why are you stopping?" I said. "She's fine. Aren't you, Ruth?"

Ruth moaned.

"See, she's fine. Let's just keep going. We're almost there and then I can massage her charley horse and maybe run her a hot bath. Just keep going."

By this time the van had rolled to a complete stop, and Jonah was staring at me as if he had just picked up the psycho hitchhiker from hell. He got out of the car, went around to the sliding side door and pulled it open. Ruth was lying on the floor curled up in a ball, panting.

"Charley horse, my ass," he said. "What's going on, Ruthie? What did you take? Do we need to go to a hospital?"

"Nooooo," she managed to say in between puffs. "Didn't take anything. Cabin…gotta get to the cabin."

Jonah turned to me. He was frowning, which did nothing to diminish his charm.

"Wanna tell me what's going on?" he asked.

"Not really," I said, sweat trickling down my spine. It wasn't my secret to tell, but the sight of Ruth in labor, even if it was false labor—please let it be false labor—made me want to cling to Jonah's fabulous biceps and beg him to stay with us and help with the birth.

"I'm not stupid, you know," he continued, "and neither are you. Whatever's going on, I figure you've got a plan—a good plan. But I'm her brother, and I'm here, and I want to help. I'm not going to run to Pete and Peggy. You should know that."

Another groan and a gasp from the backseat clinched it for me.

"She's in labor," I blurted out. "At least she thinks she is. We need to get to the cabin and get set up. I've got it all under control. She's not due for a few days, but we can't take a chance. So let's go. Now."

Jonah didn't waste any time arguing. "Get in the back with her," he barked as he jumped into the driver's seat and revved the engine. We laid rubber as he got back onto the highway. Ruth cried quietly on the floor of the van.

"It hurts so bad," she whimpered. "So bad."

"I know, sweetie, I know." I crouched down behind her and rubbed her back. The stopwatch I'd bought for timing her contractions was buried in one of my bags, so I tried counting seconds, but my brain had frozen. If she'd really been in labor for three hours, and her contractions were ten minutes apart, how long did we have before she was fully dilated? It was like one of those ridiculous math problems: John and Jim are going to Moose Jaw from Winnipeg. If John takes a train going ninety-seven miles per hour and Jim rides his bike at fourteen miles an hour, where will Jim cross the tracks and get flattened by the train? She could have the baby in ten minutes or ten hours. I prayed for ten hours.

"You okay back there?" Jonah's voice floated over us.

Ruth yelped and started to pant. I panted with her. And counted.

"She's having another contraction. I think it's only been about seven minutes since the last one. How close are we?"

"Twenty minutes, maybe fifteen, if we're lucky," Jonah said. "Are you sure about the hospital?"

"No hospital," Ruth wailed as the contraction carried her away.

Three contractions, one bruised shin (she kicked me), eight blasphemies, seventeen obscenities and numerous blows to my upper body later, we reached the cabin. Ruth managed to walk as far as the front steps, where she collapsed in tears.

"I can't do this. It's too hard," she sobbed.

Without a word, Jonah put down the stuff he was carrying and scooped Ruth up in his arms. I unlocked the door, ran into the cabin ahead of him and found a bedroom that looked as if it had been decorated by a blind nun obsessed with New Kids on the Block. Wood paneling, orange burlap curtains, lots of crucifixes, a single bed and at least ten posters of NKOTB. The most attractive thing in the room was a stupid poster of a kitten that said *Hang in there*. It was taped up next to one of the crucifixes. A deeply appropriate thought, all things considered.

We manhandled Ruth onto the bed just as another contraction hit. Jonah stayed with her (she didn't hit him at all) and I lugged all my crap in from the van. I dug my stopwatch out and handed it to Jonah.

"Time them," I said. "How long, how far apart. Rub her back. Remind her to breathe. Don't let her push. And put these rubber sheets on the bed."

Jonah nodded and grinned. "You're hot when you're bossy, you know," he said.

"Save it," I replied, grinning back. "We've got a baby to deliver."

Nine

No one remembers her beginnings.

—Rita Mae Brown, *Rubyfruit Jungle*

I bought a water-damaged copy of *Rubyfruit Jungle* from a thrift store when I was thirteen. There was a pretty red and purple flower on the cover, and above it floated the words *A novel about being different and loving it*. At thirteen, everyone thinks they're different, but they usually don't love it. I thought I might learn something from Rita Mae Brown, whoever she was. And learn I did. For about six months after I read *Rubyfruit*, I wanted to be Molly Bolt—gay, unashamed, opinionated, artistic, original. I wanted, like Molly, to have sex with a hot cheerleader and inspire the adoration of rich and powerful women. I hadn't bargained on my unremitting crush on Jonah and the fact that no cheerleader in our school seemed to be a closet dyke. I gave up on trying to be gay, but I've never forgotten how unapologetic Molly was about the circumstances of her birth. She says, "Who cares how you get here? I don't care. I really don't care. I got myself born, that's what counts. I'm here." I hoped and prayed that Ruth's baby would feel the same way. And I knew Ruth and Jonah and I would never forget this baby's beginnings.

Ruth's baby was born just before midnight, six long hours after we arrived at the cabin. Jonah stayed with us the whole time, after phoning Pete and Peggy to tell them he'd decided to go on retreat with us. Of course they were thrilled. Obviously going to Bible boot camp had worked some sort of miracle. They wouldn't have been so thrilled had they known there were only two beds in the cabin and their pregnant daughter was about to give birth to their first grandchild on one of them.

It turned out to be a pretty straightforward birth, although I certainly didn't realize it at the time. My head was full of disastrous scenarios: breech birth, strangulation by umbilical cord, hemorrhaging, loss of bowel control, stillbirth, birth defects, vaginal ripping—the list went on and on, but none of those things happened. The labor was longer than any of us liked—Ruth kept moaning, "You never told me it would take this long"—but shorter than a lot of first births. Jonah and I moved every possible projectile away from the bed when Ruth was in transition. I did everything I could to keep her comfortable and calm:

I gave her ice cubes to suck (she spat them at me) and juice to drink (ditto); I turned on the music she had chosen for the delivery (she yelled at me to turn it off); I wiped her face with a damp cloth (she bit me); I rubbed her feet (she kicked me); I left the room (she called me back); I came back (she yelled, "Get the fuck away from me!"). Jonah massaged her back and crooned old jazz standards to her. I thought for sure that she'd belt him when he sang "What a Wonderful World," but she just sobbed and bleated, "You're the best brother ever." Every few minutes I checked her dilation, and when I finally saw the baby's head (at about the same time that Ruth screamed, "My crotch is on fire!"), I let her push and the baby entered the world. In a few seconds she too was screaming at the top of her lungs. Like mother, like daughter.

Jonah caught the baby, and I think it's safe to say that we all experienced that moment of utter awe that I had felt at Boone's birth. Awe and joy and, for me at least, terror. But there was no time for anything but making sure the baby's airways were clear (although I already knew that from all the screaming) and that she had all her bits. Fingers, toes, eyes, ears. All present and accounted for. I did a quick test called an Apgar, something Maria had done right after Boone was born, to check the baby's heart rate, breathing, movement, skin color and reflexes. All excellent. I showed Jonah where to clamp the cord, and I cut it.

"Give the baby to me." Ruth pushed herself up onto her elbows and glared over her knees at Jonah and me. "And get me something to eat."

"Cool your jets, Ruthie," Jonah said. "We're cleaning her up a bit."

"Now," Ruth bellowed, and I hastily wrapped the baby in a flannel baby blanket, popped a tiny hat on her head and handed her over. If she crapped all over Ruth, so be it. Ruth lay back on the pillows and clutched the baby to her chest. Tears slid down her cheeks and into her ears.

I couldn't stop to enjoy the moment though. The placenta had yet to arrive and, while I was massaging Ruth's back, I heard the sweet, snuffly, sucking sound that could only mean one thing. Trouble.

"Ruthie," I sighed. "We agreed. No nursing. I'll give her a bottle in a minute. No attachment, remember?"

"Fuck that," Ruth replied. "She's hungry. I'm hungry. And my tits hurt. And you told me it would help deliver that placebo thing."

I giggled and nodded. The placenta took its sweet time, and it was predictably gross when it finally slid out into the soup pot I'd found in the kitchen. No way I was touching it, let alone cooking it. "Bury it," I said to Jonah, who blanched and hurried out the back door, soup pot at arm's length. I wondered if he was regretting his decision to stay. I cleaned Ruth up with warm washcloths and double-checked to make

sure she hadn't torn during the delivery. She was so preoc-
cupied with the baby that she didn't even seem aware that
I was staring at her vagina. It's not something I ever want
to do again, believe me. Sorry, Rita Mae. I stuffed all the
bloody cloths and sheets into a black garbage bag. Was there
a washer and dryer at the cabin? I couldn't remember, but if
I had to I'd wash everything in the lake. I hated the idea of
dumping the evidence of the baby's birth in some gas station
dumpster on the way home.

"What's her name?" Ruth asked. She'd stopped shivering,
and the baby was still sucking like a mini-Hoover.

"Oh, you know...I thought I'd call her Zanzibar. Place
names are huge for babies right now. But then, so are
food names. How about Zanzibar Gumdrop?" I grinned
at her and peeled off my surgical gloves. "If she'd been a
boy, I would have named her Rataxes, after the rhino in
Babar. But seeing as she's a girl, I thought Myrtle might
be better, or Beryl."

Ruth looked down at the baby and shook her head.
"No way. She's not a Myrtle or a Hortense, and no way is
she going to be named after some South American country
or a stupid candy. She's more, I don't know...she's..."

"Jane?" I said.

At that second the baby pulled away from Ruth's breast,
and I swear she looked up at her mother and smiled.
Yeah, I know, babies that age don't smile, but whatever

it was—gas, a full tummy, the warmth of her mother's body—it did the trick.

"Jane? Just Jane?" Ruth turned the name over in her mouth like a Werther's caramel. "Jane," she repeated. She looked up at me; tears streamed down her cheeks. "Jane," she said again. A shudder ran through her then and she held Jane out to me. As I wrapped my arms around the warm damp bundle, Ruth lay back in the bed, rolled over on her side and pulled a pillow over her head. Her shoulders continued to shake, and the muffled noise of her sobs filled the room. Was it a bad thing for a baby to hear her mother cry? I didn't want to risk it, so I took Jane into the kitchen, where Jonah was making Ruth her favorite sandwich: peanut butter and mayonnaise with iceberg lettuce.

"She's pretty upset," I said as I put a microscopic diaper on Jane and eased her into a tiny sleeper decorated with teddy bears.

"Understandable," Jonah replied. He cut the sandwich into triangles and put it on a bright green tray, along with three Oreo cookies and a Pepsi. "Let me talk to her."

He took the tray into Ruth's room and shut the door behind him. I was alone with Jane, who lay quietly in my arms and squinted blearily at me, her eyelids puffy, her perfect lips opening and closing like a goldfish. She seemed fine, but what did I know? It had been so much easier when she was safely tucked away in the small wet universe inside

Ruth's belly. But now that she was here, whole new vistas of accident and pain and illness crowded my mind. What if I dropped her? What if she wouldn't suck from a bottle? What if she had an invisible illness that had to be diagnosed and treated immediately so she didn't die before her first birthday? What if she ended up with people who burned her with cigarettes and starved her and locked her in a closet?

My heart started to pound as I thought about what had just happened and what had to happen next. Jane gave a tiny burp and I looked down at her pursed lips and the sweep of her eyelashes and I shuddered. It was so different from Boone's birth. There was no nursery all ready for Jane, no cute little bassinet, no designer baby quilts. Just a wicker basket lined with an old flannel sheet. It didn't seem right or fair, but it had to be done. We'd agreed.

"She's sleeping now," Jonah said when he came out of Ruth's room. "She's pretty upset though." He paused and I could see him take in the fact that I, too, was not exactly relaxed. "You okay?" he asked. "You look pretty stressed. I'll hold Jane if you like."

The look on my face must have said it all. That's what it's like when someone knows you really well. You can't get away with jackshit.

"Julia," he said softly. "It's gonna be okay. Jane will be fine. We'll make sure of that. Right now you need to get some rest. Uncle Jonah will look after her." He held out his arms and I walked into them, baby and all. We stood that way for a few minutes, swaying together in the kitchen, and then he gently prised Jane away from me, wrapped her in his fleece jacket and walked out onto the dark front porch. I could hear him singing "Summertime" to her as I dragged myself into the second bedroom and collapsed onto the bed. "Your daddy's rich and your momma's good-lookin'" my ass.

WHEN I WOKE UP, it was still dark, Ruth and Jonah were arguing, and Jane was wailing. I staggered into the kitchen. Jonah was sitting at the kitchen table. Jane was snuggled into the crook of his left arm and a bottle of formula was poised over her open mouth. Her face was red and contorted, not unlike her mother's. Ruth was standing over Jonah. The best word to describe her was "drenched." She was crying (could she possibly have been crying all the time I was sleeping?) and the front of her T-shirt was soaked—with tears and snot and something I knew was called colostrum, which is the super-nutritious stuff women produce right after birth.

"Give her to me," Ruth yelled.

"We talked about this," Jonah said calmly. "She needs to get used to a bottle."

"No, she doesn't." Ruth made a grab for the bottle and missed. Jane sounded as if she was in pain. Maybe she was.

"Babies pick up on emotions, you know," I said. "Jane should be hearing laughter and lullabies. She should be eating and pooping and sleeping in a cocoon of love, not a hive of anger. The sooner we give her up, the sooner she'll have all that.

"Give her to me," I said to Jonah. "Stop yelling," I said to Ruth. "It's bad for Jane."

"But, Julia…" Jonah started to argue with me, but something in my expression stopped him. He shrugged and handed Jane and the bottle to me. She stopped wailing as I wiggled the nipple into her mouth, praying that she would know what to do. Ruth collapsed into a rocking chair, sobbing and hugging her chest. The room was silent except for the squeak of the rockers. Jane wasn't sucking. She turned her head away from the nipple every time I put it near her lips. After a few minutes, she started to scream again. The more I tried to get her to take the bottle, the louder she screamed.

Ruth stood up and walked over to me. "She's starving, Julia. And I'm exploding. Give her to me. I never said I'd let her starve."

"She'll get used to the bottle. It only stands to reason." I looked at Jonah and he shook his head.

"Ruth's right, Julia," he said. "Starving her wasn't part of the deal."

I couldn't believe it—months of planning and sacrifice were going down the drain because my candy-assed so-called boyfriend couldn't take listening to a baby cry? I shoved the baby at Ruth and turned to leave the room. "You guys are on your own, then," I snapped. "I'm done."

"Don't be like that, Jules," Jonah said, grabbing my elbow as I stomped past him. "Just let Ruthie feed her, and we'll work something out."

"Not with me, you won't," I said. "I'm going back to sleep." The last thing I heard as I left the room was the slurpy snuffle of a happy baby. I glanced back from the doorway: Ruth's eyes were closed and a small smile—the first I'd seen in a while—had crept across her face. If I hadn't known better, I would have thought she'd done this before. I'd read all about how difficult breastfeeding can be, and I'd seen it firsthand with Miki and Boone. Boone just couldn't get the hang of it, and Miki was going out of her mind. Jane, on the other hand, latched onto Ruth's nipple like a regular milking machine. Go figure.

I MUST HAVE slept for twelve hours. When I got up, the sun was shining, and Jane was asleep in the basket I had prepared for her to be given away in. It was the kind of huge basket that hotels fill with fruit and chocolate and booze for celebrity guests. Jane deserved better, I thought; she was infinitely more precious than any bottle of hundred-year-old champagne. Her price, as they say in the Bible, was above rubies.

And yet she was a gift we had to give away. This was taking re-gifting to a whole new level.

JONAH AND I slept together the next night. And I mean slept. We didn't even take off our clothes, and I hardly thought at all about having hot monkey sex. I was still pretty pissed at him for siding with Ruth. When I woke up, he was snoring gently into my right ear. I started to get up, but he reached for me and pulled me back down.

"Ruth wants to keep her, you know," he murmured.

I nodded into his chest. "And you don't? Coulda fooled me."

He sighed. "I know all the reasons for giving her up, but...yeah. It seems wrong to give her away. Really wrong. I mean...she's blood, Jules. My blood. Ruth's. Mom and Dad's."

"But they won't let Ruth keep her. You know that."

"I know," he said. "But I don't think Ruth's going to give her up without a fight. And maybe not even then."

He rolled onto his back and stretched. I laid my head on his chest and listened to his heart. When Jane started to cry in the next room, his heart speeded up. So did mine. He'd fallen in love—with a baby. I wondered where that left me.

FOR THE NEXT ten days, Ruth and Jonah worshipped the mini-goddess they called JJ—for Just Jane, I guess. I still called her Jane. They followed her rhythm of sleeping, waking and eating; they marveled at the fact that her poo didn't stink; they sang the praises of her magnificent appetite and her ability to burp on demand; they made her a crown of wildflowers and a shrine of candles in empty formula bottles. Jonah fashioned a cool baby sling out of a blanket and took her for walks by the lake while Ruth slept. Every three hours, like clockwork, Jane ate. At night Jonah was with me, but he was too tired to do much more than kiss me before he fell asleep. I read and slept and took solitary swims in the lake while Jonah cooked, washed dishes and did the laundry.

There was a lovely dreamy quality to those days, even though Ruth and I weren't actually talking. I knew none of it would last—my anger, the silence between me and Ruth, the nights with Jonah—but it was summer and we were teenagers at a lake without our parents. Ruth went swimming, her belly and boobs exploding out of her bikini as she cannonballed off the dock. She bathed Jane in a dishpan and dried her with a sun-warmed towel. When Jane's little umbilical cord stump fell off, Ruth made a necklace out of it with a piece of string.

I knew there was no way Ruth was giving Jane up. She adored her. So did Jonah. So did I, for that matter, but it didn't stop me from trying to convince Ruth to change her mind.

I finally gave up when Ruth tossed the van keys to Jonah and told him to drive me to the nearest town so I could catch a bus home.

"Stop being such a bitch, Julia," she said. "I'm keeping JJ, and I don't need you telling me what a bad idea it is. I know this isn't what we planned, but it's what I want. So either suck it up or fuck off." She glared at me. "Did it ever occur to you that this isn't about you? You can walk away any time you like. So do it. Go make other plans, 'cause I'm done having you make mine. Yeah, I know everything's gone sideways on you, but that's when the fun begins. When things get interesting. But that's not the Julia Riley way, is it?"

"Okay, okay," I said. "I get it. I don't happen to agree"—Ruth rolled her eyes—"but I'd still like to stay, if that's okay with you."

Ruth and Jonah exchanged glances and Ruth nodded. "On two conditions," she said.

"What's that?"

"You let me give JJ a middle name."

I nodded.

"And you take the pole out of your butt."

RUTH HAD A few days when she was restless and irritable, but her baby blues didn't last. She couldn't get enough of

Jane, and Jane, in return, was the most contented baby on earth. Ruth sang to her—"Hush little baby, don't say a word, Mama's going to buy you a red T-bird"—and told her weird stories about a talking gopher named Dr. Ramos. Jane seemed to love it all. Ruth was a natural-born mother. Who knew? I still didn't think she should keep Jane, but I kept my mouth shut and the pole out of my ass. I was surprisingly comfortable.

"I'm really good at this, aren't I?" she said a few days before we were due to leave the cabin in the second week of August. We were all sitting around the kitchen watching Jane blow bubbles. I highly recommend it as a way to pass an evening, by the way. Beats reality television, for sure.

"So, what's the plan?" I asked. Ruth shifted Jane onto her shoulder and patted her back. Jane obliged with a belch that would make a frat boy proud.

"Go home. Face the music. See how Pete and Peggy react," Jonah said.

Ruth snorted. "Wow. Awesome plan. Wish I'd thought of it myself."

Jonah got up and went outside, where we could see him pacing the porch.

"What do you suggest, then?" I asked. "You can't just disappear with her. You have to go home sometime."

"I'm not giving her up." Ruth glared at me and I held my hands up, palms out.

"You're preaching to the choir, sister."

"I'm not so sure," Ruth said. "At least Jonah loves JJ. He's even been talking about delaying going to cooking school."

My eyes widened. "He'd do that for you?"

"Yup," she said.

"Wow. No way you should let him, but wow."

"Yeah, but he doesn't go for another month anyway, so he'll help me out with Pete and Peggy. Maybe they'll surprise me."

I gave a short bark of a laugh. "Only if you tell them it was an immaculate conception."

Ten

"Where's Papa going with that axe?"
—E.B. White, *Charlotte's Web*

I have read *Charlotte's Web* once a year, on my birthday, since I was eight. I never get tired of it. If I ever have a son, I'm going to name him Wilbur. Okay, maybe not his first name, but his second for sure. At first I loved the pictures almost as much as I loved the story, but mostly I love the way it's written. E.B. White never uses more or bigger words than he has to. He writes about really important things like birth and death, the love between true friends, the value of imagination, but he's got a sense of humor about it all. For a while I went around saying "Salutations!" instead of "Hello," until my mother threatened to take the book away. I learned the names for the seven sections of a spider's leg from *Charlotte's Web*. I also learned the meaning of the words *languishing* and *spinnerets* and *gullible*. Charlotte saves Wilbur's life with words: *Some Pig, Radiant, Terrific* and finally *Humble*. As Ruth and Jane and Jonah and I drove back from the lake, I wondered if there were any words that could save Ruth from the wrath of her parents. I didn't think a sign over Jane's head that said *Some Baby* would work, but we had to do something—Ruth, Jonah and me. We'd talked of nothing else for days, but short of a miracle—like Pete and Peggy suddenly becoming decent, loving, sane parents— we hadn't come up with anything more original than presenting a united front.

"Maybe they'll see her and fall in love, like we did," Ruth said dreamily from the backseat, where she was nursing Jane.

Jonah and I glanced at each other; he raised his eyebrows. I shrugged and crossed my eyes. Ruth was obviously in some hormonal la-la land. We were twenty minutes away from her house, and I wanted to puke. We planned to go in together and, if necessary, protect Ruth and Jane from the axe of Pastor Pete's sure-to-be-biblical judgment. Unlike Fern's father in *Charlotte's Web*, I couldn't see Pastor Pete's eyes brimming with tears at the sight of this brand-new miracle. I couldn't see Peggy welcoming Jane into her house the way Fern's mother welcomed Wilbur. Jane would be an embarrassment to them, a betrayal of their beliefs, a source of shame and ridicule. Pete would act like Ruth was a whore, and Peggy, good Christian wife that she is, would back him up. Our plan was to give them a chance to do the right thing, and if they didn't, we'd go to my house. That was it. The grand plan. I had called my mother to let her know I was on my way home. I had neglected to tell her I might not be alone.

We pulled into Ruth's driveway and parked behind Peggy's old beige Toyota. Pete was mowing the lawn.

"Shit," said Ruth. "They're home. We're screwed."

She looked ill, as if she'd only just that minute realized what we were about to face. Jane was in her basket beside Ruth on the backseat and she started to stir and whimper. In a couple of minutes, her siren wail would cut through the sound of the lawn mower, and the shitstorm would rain down. Jonah started to unload the van, and I got out to help Ruth with Jane. The front door opened, and Peggy came out just as Pete turned off the mower and bounded over to the van. Their collective double take was priceless, like a cartoon. They literally recoiled when they saw what was in the basket. Pete almost fell on his ass.

"What's that?" Peggy screeched.

"Duh, Mom," Ruth said. "What does it look like? A basket of apples?"

"It's a baby. I can see that, missy." Peggy turned to Pete as Ruth mouthed the word *missy* at me and rolled her eyes. "Pete, say something. Do something." She wrung her hands. Really.

Pete looked from Jane to Ruth to Jonah and back again to Ruth.

"All I can say, young lady, is that better not be yours." Even as he said it, I could see that he knew better. "And you, son," he said, glaring at Jonah, "what did you have to do with this?"

Before Jonah could reply, Jane started to scream. She wasn't used to waiting for her meals. Neither was Ruth. Her T-shirt was soaked. She took Jane out of the basket and headed for the front door. "I don't know about you," she said over her shoulder, "but I'm pretty sure the neighbors don't need to see my tits. I'm going inside. Jane's hungry." Jonah and I walked with her, one on either side.

Just as we reached the door, Pete charged in front of us, planted himself in the doorway, flung his arms wide and gripped the doorframe. "Jezebel!" he hissed. "You shall not enter my home. You shall not defile it with your filthiness and the evidence of your fornication."

It was our turn to recoil, as much from the spittle that sprayed out of his mouth as from his words.

"Dad," Jonah said, "take it easy. If she goes, I go too."

Behind us I could hear Peggy gasp. Now's the time, Peggy, I thought. Stand up for your daughter. Tell Pete to go to hell. Stop wringing your hands, and slap him before I do.

"The great whore of Babylon sitteth upon many waters and the inhabitants of the earth have been made drunk with the wine of her fornication," Peggy shrieked. So much for standing up for her daughter. I covered Jane's ears. "How dare you bring your bastard here," she continued. "And you," she turned to me, "I blame you for this. You have poisoned our daughter against us and against her faith, and hellfire awaits you."

"Thanks," I said. "I figure hell must be an improvement over what's happening here. C'mon, Ruth. This is bad for Jane." Ruth was doing a lame imitation of Lot's wife, so I grabbed her arm and propelled her back to the van. Jonah stayed with his parents. Jane was screeching so loudly that I couldn't hear what he was saying to them, but I think it was along the lines of "See ya, losers."

Pete grabbed him with both hands, and Jonah shook him off as if he were a flake of dandruff. When Peggy fell on her knees and wrapped her arms around his legs, he very gently extricated himself and stepped away from her.

"I'll bring the van back later," he said. "Once Ruthie's settled somewhere." The last thing I saw as we drove away was Pete turning his back on Peggy as she knelt in the driveway, her hands over her face.

"That was harsh," I said to Ruth as she nursed Jane. "You okay?"

"Yeah," Ruth said. "They're such assholes. They didn't even look at her. How could they not even look at her? Their own grandchild." A tear splashed onto Jane's nose and she blinked and hiccuped. Ruth laughed but the tears kept falling. "They're so fucking predictable. 'Jezebel.' 'Great Whore of Babylon.' Jesus. If they'd only look at her. She's just a baby. It's not her fault."

"It's gonna be okay, Ruth. My mom will help. She loves babies." I wasn't actually sure if that was true, never having seen my mom with a baby, but I knew she loved Ruth—and me. And she wasn't inclined to spew nasty bits of scripture either, even when she was mad. The worst thing she ever said was "To everything there is a season" when I asked if I could get my ears pierced. Come to think of it, she's said that a lot over the years. It's basically her way of saying no, without actually saying it.

When we got to my place, Jonah parked, helped us load our stuff into the elevator and announced he was going to wait in the van.

"I'm going to shut my eyes, listen to some tunes. Your place is small, and I'll just get in the way."

Yeah, right, I thought. You can't look my mom in the eye when you've been sleeping with her daughter for two weeks. Even though we didn't have sex. We slept beside each other like brother and sister, too exhausted to do much more than kiss. Well, okay, we did a bit more than kiss, but still. My virtue remained intact, unfortunately. The best birth control in the world is a screaming baby in the next room.

Ruth and I rode up in the elevator in silence; Jane was still snuffling at Ruth's breast. I opened the door to the apartment and called out, "We're here!" and my mom ran out of the living room with a huge smile on her face.

"It's so good to see you, sweetie," she said. "And you too, Ruth. I've missed you guys." Her gaze took in Jane. I held my breath, but she didn't miss a beat. "And who have we here?" she said softly, pulling the flannel blanket away from Jane's face.

I don't think I've ever loved my mother more, or been prouder of her, than I was at that moment. Suddenly I understood what *walking the walk* meant.

"JJ," said Ruth. "This is…my daughter JJ."

"For Jane," I added. "Just Jane."

"She's beautiful," said my mom. "But a little smelly. Let's get her cleaned up and put her down for a nap. Then it's tuna-melt time, I think. You both look a little…wan. And isn't Jonah with you?"

"In the van. Outside," I mumbled.

"Oh, for heaven's sake, Julia. Go get him." She put her arm around Ruth and Jane and led them away. I could hear her running the tap in the bathroom and chattering to Ruth as I went downstairs. I was sure we'd get around to discussing what had happened, but as my mom says— To everything there is a season.

AFTER DINNER RUTH fell asleep on the couch with Jane in her basket on the floor beside her. Jonah did the dishes while

I sat at the kitchen table with my mother and told her the whole story. She was silent as I talked. No questions. No comments. No scriptural outbursts. She did frown a bit, and when I was finished, she remained silent for a couple of minutes. Even though there were no outward signs, I was pretty sure she was praying. Finally she said, "I'm not sure what to say, Julia. Obviously it hasn't worked out the way you thought it would, but then, what does?" A rueful smile turned up the corners of her mouth. "Nobody knows that better than me. But I'm proud of you. You looked after your friend, even if your reasons and your methods are slightly… um…unorthodox. Ruth seems physically fine, thanks to you, and the baby is lovely and clearly happy and healthy. But you know I have to call Pete and Peggy and tell them Ruth's here. They must be worried sick."

I snorted. They were sick, but not with worry.

"I know, I know," she said. "But give them a chance to get used to the idea. Maybe they'll come around. No matter what, they deserve to know where she is."

"No, they don't, Mom," I said. "They don't deserve anything. You should have heard them. Peggy called her the Whore of Babylon. Pete barred the door. It was totally disgusting."

"I'll tell them." Jonah spoke from the doorway, where he stood drying his hands. "I have to take the van back anyway, and then I'm going to head over to Sean's house."

Sarah N. Harvey

"Tell them we'll talk tomorrow, then," said my mom. Jonah nodded, thanked my mother for dinner, kissed the top of my head and took off.

"He's a lovely boy," Mom said.

"Yeah," I muttered. "Maybe too lovely." For the last two weeks, Jonah had been everything a girl could want: sensitive, caring, helpful, kind. Good to his sister; fabulous with his niece. His zit had cleared up, and I was feeling mean and grubby in the face of his calm perfection. I mean, as far as I could tell, he didn't even fart under the covers or scratch his balls. And now he was sucking up to my mom.

"Go to bed, Julia," my mom said. "You must be exhausted. Everything will look different in the morning, even Jonah." She patted my cheek and pointed down the hall to my room. "Remember what Scarlett O'Hara said."

"'As God is my witness, I'll never be hungry again'?" I replied in a fake southern accent.

Mom laughed, and Jane whimpered in her basket.

"No, silly," Mom whispered. "Scarlett said, 'Tomorrow is another day.' Go get some sleep."

It wasn't until I had undressed and slipped between the cool sheets that I realized my mother had nowhere to sleep, but I was too tired and, let's face it, too selfish, to get up and offer her my bed. The next thing I knew it was morning, and I could hear Jane crying. I pulled on some sweatpants and went out to the kitchen, where Mom was circling the

kitchen table with a wailing Jane in her arms. I could hear
the shower running.

"Ruth thought she had time for a shower before Jane woke
up," Mom said, patting Jane's back and jigging up and down.

"I'll take her if you like," I said. "You look really tired."
I held my arms out for Jane, who quieted briefly and then
started crying again when she realized I wasn't Ruth. How
do babies know these things? Smell? Boob size? I waltzed her
around the kitchen while my mom made coffee and toast.
Jane prefers the waltz to the samba or the two-step. Less
bouncy, I guess. "Sorry about last night. You could have
slept in my bed, you know."

"I know. I made a little nest on the floor. Camping
foamie, sleeping bag, couple of pillows. It was fine. I wanted
you to sleep."

"Thanks," I said. Ruth came out of the shower, a towel
wrapped around her head and an old bathrobe of my mother's barely covering her butt. She sat down at the kitchen
table, bared a breast and took Jane from me.

"Greedy little piggy," she murmured, brushing her lips
over Jane's soft spot.

JONAH PHONED ME from his friend Sean's just after breakfast.

"I talked to Mom and Dad again," he said. He didn't
sound happy.

"Uh-huh. Let me guess. They take it all back and they're going to welcome Ruth and Jane with open arms."

"Not so much," he said. "I think Pete's exact words were, 'Your sister is dead to me.'"

"He actually said that?" I shrieked, and Ruth glanced up from nursing Jane. The look she gave me was full of pain. And understanding. I scanned the table for possible missiles, but Ruth made no move toward the saltshaker or the jar of jam. All her most diva-like behavior seemed to have been buried at the cottage along with her placenta. It was weird—I almost wanted the old Ruth back, even if it meant stitches.

"Give me the phone," she said calmly. I handed it over and stood back. She had thrown phones before and with far less provocation.

"Yo, Bro," she said. "Talk to me." She listened for a minute, nodded and handed the phone back to me. "He wants to talk to you again."

I held the phone at arm's length as I stared in amazement at Ruth. As if in answer to my unspoken questions, Ruth said, "I've got better things to do than flip out over those assholes. Talk to Jonah. Right now we're going to have a bath, aren't we, Jane?" As she left the kitchen, Jane cradled in her arms, she stopped in front of me. "Your Aunty Julia loves you, Jane," she said, as she lifted Jane up for me to kiss. "She'll figure something out."

"Julia? Julia? Are you there?" Jonah's faint voice startled me out of my trance.

I put the phone to my ear. "Yeah, Jonah, I'm here. But I don't know what to do."

"C'mon, Julia. You always have a plan, even if you don't like to admit it. Plan A, Plan B, Plan Z. It's the Julia Riley way. You could give workshops: Loving Your Inner List-Maker. And I know you're glad Ruth kept her."

Whoa! What had Jonah taken with his juice this morning?

"What do you mean, I'm glad Ruth kept her? Haven't you been paying attention? The whole idea was to keep it all under wraps so Ruth could finish school, leave town, carry on with her life."

"Carry on with *your* life, you mean," Jonah said. "Things changed. Ruth changed. You've changed."

I opened my mouth to protest, but he kept right on talking. "I think you got attached long before JJ was born, otherwise you would have figured out how to get back from the cottage without anyone knowing there was a baby. That's one part of it you never talked about. If I hadn't been there, how were you going to get home? I've been thinking about this a lot."

I started to splutter but he cut me off again. "I think being at Boone's birth made you wonder about keeping JJ. And when Ruth suddenly turned into Super-Mom, you hardly objected at all. I'm not saying it's a bad thing—but you might as well come clean. You wanted Ruth to keep her, but you couldn't admit it. You knew Pete and Peggy would freak, therefore you must have another plan. Some things never change. Julia Riley always has a plan."

I was silent for a minute—long enough for him to think I'd hung up on him. When I finally spoke, all I said was, "You're right—about a lot of things. But you're wrong about a plan. I don't have a plan. I don't even have a list. But I do have an idea."

Eleven

Dorothy lived in the midst of the great Kansas prairies,
with Uncle Henry, who was a farmer, and Aunt Em, who
was the farmer's wife.
— L. Frank Baum, *The Wonderful Wizard of Oz*

There are an awful lot of dead parents in children's books.
Mothers get shot by hunters or they die in childbirth,
fathers drown or are killed in faraway wars. Flaming car
wrecks on winding mountain roads claim their share of
blameless moms and dads. It's a dangerous business, being a
parent. In contemporary books there is a ton of emotional
abandonment, if not actual death. I'm not sure which is
worse, never having experienced either. I can't remember
what happened to Dorothy Gale's parents, but Uncle Henry
and Aunt Em were her family, and she loved them. When
all was said and done—witches, Munchkins, yellow brick
roads, flying monkeys, scarecrows, tin men, lions and
wizards—all she wanted to do was go home to boring, flat
Kansas. But Ruth couldn't tap her heels together three times

and be magically transported to a home where she and
her daughter would be wrapped in hugs and covered with
kisses. Her parents were dead. Maybe not physically, but in
any way that mattered to Ruth and Jane. They definitely
weren't in Kansas anymore.

My mom was a star about having Ruth and Jane in our
apartment, but after three nights of sleeping on the foamie
in the dining room, I regretted telling Mom to take my
bed. We all knew the arrangement was temporary, but even
so, I really needed some space. I guess my mom did too,
because she took me aside while Ruth was bathing Jane and
said, "I talked to Pete and Peggy again. They won't even
consider having Ruth come home. And they call themselves Christians." She practically spat the last bit. "I'll never
understand it." She sighed and continued, "I talked to some
people at the church, and there's a home for girls in Ruth's
situation. It's called Hope House and it's—"

I started to protest and she said, "Hear me out, Julia.
Just hear me out."

I nodded and stayed silent, fuming. Hope House, my ass.
No way were Ruth and Jane going into a home for unwed
mothers. No way. I'd get a job and rent us an apartment first.

"It's a nice place," my mother was saying. "Not too far
away. You'd be able to drive up on weekends to see her."

"What!" I yelled. "Weekends? Mom, Ruth's almost my
sister. Jane's, like, my niece. We can't just send them away.

Ruth needs me. Jane needs me. Can't they stay here for a while longer? I don't mind sleeping on the floor, and I'll help out more, I really will."

"It's not that, Julia. You're a big help, but you'll be back in school soon," my mother said wearily. "And this apartment's way too small. Ruth and Jane need a room of their own at the very least. They'll get that at Hope House—along with counseling and the chance for Ruth to finish high school by correspondence."

"She won't go," I said. "She'll run away. You know she will. And we'll be the ones who put her and Jane on the street." Even as I said it, my stomach started to churn. Where would she go? I shuddered at the thought of Ruth and Jane on a bus to Vancouver—no money, nowhere to stay, hooking up with street people. "I'm working on something else, Mom. Please—just give me a few more days."

"Something else, huh?" She gazed at me appraisingly and nodded. "Just a few days, then. I'll tell the people at Hope House that she's okay here for now."

"Thanks, Mom," I said. "And thanks for being so great about all this." I waved my arm to take in the baby blankets and sleepers and boxes of diapers that were strewn around the living room.

"She's a lovely baby," my mom said, "and I'm enjoying having them here. But if you think you're going to quit school and go to work to support them, just put that idea out of your mind right now. Nobody's life is going to get ruined by this. Nobody's. Least of all yours."

What is it with mothers and mind reading? Time for Plan B. Or was it Plan C?

MARIA'S CAR WAS in the driveway and the front door was open when I went over to my dad's house the weekend after we came back from the cabin. Even though it was blazing hot outside, the slate floor of the hallway was cool on my bare feet. Cool and kind of gritty, like no one had washed or even swept it for a long time. A stack of newspapers was piled up inside the front door alongside a lot of empty wine bottles. A lot. Obviously recycling wasn't a top priority either. Maybe everyone was too drunk. But nursing mothers weren't supposed to drink, were they? So that left my dad, who wasn't usually much of a drinker.

I shrugged and walked to the kitchen, where take-out containers covered the counters and dirty dishes filled the sink. The kitchen table was heaped with unopened mail, half-filled baby bottles, wads of used tissue, five coffee mugs with mould growing in them and a contraption that looked kind of like a bicycle horn. On closer examination, it turned out to be a breast pump. A quick peek into the living room revealed more chaos—baskets of stinky laundry, a stroller lying on its side, more dirty dishes.

There was a nasty smell in the house—sort of sour and sad, as if the windows hadn't been opened in weeks.

I called out as I went up the stairs, and Maria stuck her head out of Miki and Dad's bedroom. "In here," she whispered. "Boone's sleeping. Miki's down in that little room again."

I tiptoed into the bedroom and gagged. It was stifling and smelled like rotten fish; the curtains were drawn against the summer sun, and all the lights were off. I could make out my dad in the rocker, with Boone asleep in his arms. Maria was tidying—throwing little sleepers into a basket, stuffing used diapers into a garbage bag. I bent over to kiss my dad and he whispered, "Give Maria a hand, okay? We'll talk later."

I nodded, took a laundry basket from Maria and headed downstairs to the laundry room. Maria joined me a few minutes later, dragging two full garbage bags.

"What's going on, Maria?" I asked as I started the first load of laundry.

"Miki's having some problems," she said. "I thought she was okay—she never called and I got busy—all my babies came at once. Your dad called this morning."

"What kind of problems?" I asked as I loaded the dishwasher. Maria hauled the bags of garbage to the back door and started filling another bag with half-full cartons of what looked like congealed pad thai.

"Problems feeding the baby, problems with her moods, problems with anxiety."

"But she seemed so happy before," I said. "I mean, she was okay for a while, wasn't she?"

"Yes," Maria replied, "at first everything was fine. She had some problems feeding Boone, but lots of first-time mothers struggle with that."

I thought of Jane at Ruth's breast—the ease and contentment blazing on Ruth's face. Ruth had told me it was the best feeling she'd ever had. Way better than sex. I hoped that part wasn't true.

Maria continued. "I checked up on her fairly regularly, and I knew she was having a hard time, but she was adamant that she wanted to keep trying to nurse him. I don't need to tell you, Miki's a pretty determined woman. I didn't have any reason to think she and Boone wouldn't get the hang of it. A couple of days ago your dad realized that Boone was starving. Crying all the time, even when Miki tried to nurse him. Then Miki refused to nurse him at all, and she locked herself away in that little room. Your dad has been trying to cope ever since. But Boone isn't taking to the bottle too well either."

"Is Boone okay?" A vision of my baby brother laid out in a tiny coffin, wizened like a prune, took my breath away.

Maria put her hand on my arm. "Yes, Julia, he's okay. A little underweight, but he'll be fine as soon as he gets the hang of the bottle. It won't take long, I'm sure. Today was better than yesterday. I'm more worried about Miki, to be honest."

I glared at her as I ran water over the dishes in the sink. "Why? She's the grown-up. Boone's the helpless one." Even as I said it I knew it was unfair, but I didn't care. Helpless adults are scary. I needed Miki to get better. Not just for Boone, but for Ruth and Jane. And for Dad.

"How have you been?" Maria asked. It was pretty clear that she wasn't going to debate Miki's fitness to be a mother. "I hear you and Ruth were up at the lake. Must have been fun."

There wasn't even the tiniest hint of sarcasm or irony in Maria's voice, nor was there a smirk on her face. I figured everyone must know about Jane by now, but Maria was clearly out of the loop. I took a deep breath and said, "Well, if you call being a midwife to your best friend fun, then, yeah, it was fun."

Maria dropped the dirty coffee cup she had been holding. Fortunately, its fall was broken by a bag full of dirty diapers.

"You delivered a baby? Ruth's baby? By yourself?" Maria sat down hard on a kitchen chair. She grimaced and pulled a pizza box out from under her and threw it to the floor.

"Yup," I said, suddenly feeling as proud as if I'd given birth myself. "A baby girl named Jane. Ruth calls her JJ.

She's awesome. And Ruth—Ruth is an amazing mother. And Jonah helped."

"You're pretty amazing yourself, I'd say," Maria replied. Her eyes narrowed. "All that stuff about school reports—total bullshit, yes?"

"Yeah, but I really was—am—interested. A new life, helping that happen. It's pretty cool."

"Yeah, it is," she said. "But you took a lot of chances. What if the baby had been breech? What if…"

"I know…I thought of all those things too. But her parents would have sent her away. They still want to send her away. So does my mom."

"Send who away?" Neither of us had heard my dad come into the kitchen. He was standing in the doorway, scratching his stubble and looking from me to Maria and back again. "Send who away?" he repeated.

"Ruth," I said. "And Jane."

"Who's Jane?"

Maria got up and started stuffing garbage in bags again while I made Dad some coffee and told him everything that had happened. When I was finished—well, not quite finished—all he said was "Wow." I carried on with the cleanup as he sat and drank his coffee. Gradually some order rose out of the chaos: the counter reappeared, sticky with blobs of peanut butter and gritty with spilled sugar, and I scoured it clean; the stink of shit and piss and tears and sweat was replaced by the perfume of Javex and Sunlight and Mr. Clean. Through it all, my dad sat and sipped his coffee. When he was done, he got up, gave me a hug and said, "I have to go check on Boone. We'll talk later. I'm glad you're here."

"Me too, Dad," I said as he turned to go upstairs. "Um, Dad? Can Ruth and Jane and I stay here for a while?"

He paused with his foot on the first step. "You don't ever have to ask my permission to stay here, Julia. You should know that. But Ruth and Jane? I don't know. What does your mother say?" he said.

I swallowed hard. He'd never asked me that before. About anything. "She said Ruth and Jane had to go somewhere called Hope House unless I could figure something else out. She's been great," I added, "but our place is too small. And you've got extra bedrooms and I can help Miki with Boone and Jane's a really good baby and Ruth is different—"

He held up his hand like a traffic cop. "Stop, Julia. I get it. It's fine. You can come." He smiled for the first time since I'd gotten there, but there was no joy in it. "It can't get much worse than this, can it? Just give me a day to break it to Miki. Not that she'll care. As long as someone else looks after Boone, she wouldn't care if the combined casts of *Cats* and *The Phantom of the Opera* moved in."

It was my turn to say "Wow," but not because Miki hated *Cats* and every other musical by Andrew Lloyd Webber.

I totally got that. No, I said "Wow" because I had never ever, not once, heard my dad sound so bitter.

TWO DAYS LATER, Jonah drove Ruth, Jane and me over to my dad's. I didn't plan on staying very long—a couple of nights, max—but I wanted to get Ruth and Jane settled and make sure Boone was okay before I went back to Mom's. She'd agreed to my plan on three conditions: that Miki and Dad really were okay with it; that I not sacrifice school for playing house; and that the minute the arrangement became a problem for anyone, Ruth and Jane would go to Hope House. She and Dad talked on the phone—and yes, I listened in on my extension— but he didn't back out and she didn't preach at him, so, all things considered, it was a success as divorced parent conversations go. Mom asked about Miki, and Dad's voice broke a little when he told her that Miki spent all day in a small dark room, crying.

"It's definitely postpartum depression, Sharon," he said. "If not psychosis. I know it. Everyone knows it—her doctor, the midwife, the public health nurse. But Miki won't take anything for it. She won't talk to me. She won't even look at Boone. She says she's not good for him." He sounded like he was about to cry, and I imagined him sitting at the kitchen table, unshaven, in grubby jeans, surrounded by dirty dishes.

It broke my heart, and from the tone of my mother's voice, it was getting to her too.

"Poor thing," she said. "Miki, I mean," she added quickly. Not fast enough, Mom, I thought. I heard it; I'm sure Dad heard it. A hint of ex-wifely concern, a distinct thawing in the chilly atmosphere of their relationship. It didn't last. When she spoke again, she was brisk and businesslike. "Julia's idea is that Ruth can help out in exchange for her room and board. Jane's a very easy baby, so it shouldn't be a problem. Ruth knows what's expected of her, and Julia will come on the usual days once school starts. For now she can be there as much as she likes. She can give Ruth a break if she needs it."

"Okay," Dad said. There was a pause. "Uh, Sharon? I really appreciate this."

Mom laughed. A miracle. "You *appreciate* having a teenage mother and her newborn baby come to stay with you when your wife is depressed and you're going nuts looking after her and the baby? Pete and Peggy should be on their knees thanking God that some people know how to do the right thing. And I *do* thank you for taking her in."

"You're welcome," Dad said. "But I meant I appreciate you talking to me. It helps."

"I'm glad," Mom said. She took a breath.

Don't say it, Mom, I thought. Don't say *I'm praying for you* or *If God brings you to it, He will bring you through it.*

I squeezed my eyes shut, just like I used to do when I was little and I had to take cough syrup.

"I'm happy to help" was all she said. "We'll just have to take it a day at a time. Give Boone a kiss for me."

She hung up, but Dad was still on the line.

"Holy shit," he said reverently before he hung up. My sentiments exactly.

WHEN WE GOT to Dad's, he was in the kitchen singing to Boone while he burped him. The song of the day was "Don't Worry Baby." A bizarre selection, given that it's about a guy and his car. Never too early to start the indoctrination, I guess.

"Hey, Julia," he said as we walked in. "Boone's holding out on me. Wanna give it a shot?"

"Sure," I said. I put my pack down on a chair and took Boone from him. "But I'm not singing some lame-ass Beach Boys' song to him." I started to waltz around the room humming "Edelweiss," of all things. What can I say? I love *The Sound of Music*. Always have. When we were little, Ruth always insisted on being both Captain von Trapp and Maria in our bedroom productions. Jonah, if we could talk him into it, had the thankless role of Rolf the Nazi boy as well as all the male von Trapp children. I was all the nuns and all the girls. Today I was the Captain—firm, sensitive, musically gifted. Ruth came in with Jane, followed by Jonah, who was loaded down like a Sherpa. A hot white Sherpa in Tommy Hilfiger jeans and a tight T-shirt. I stopped singing. The biceps were very distracting.

"Where should I put these, sir?" he asked my dad.

Dad gestured up the stairs. "Third door on the left, past the bathroom."

Jonah nodded and disappeared up the stairs, with Ruth and Jane behind him. I had just launched into a passionate rendition of "Do-Re-Mi," when Boone let loose with a huge belch. About a gallon of formula cascaded down the front of my shirt.

"Crap," I said, reaching for a towel.

"That comes later," Dad said. "He's pretty much mastered the sucking part. Now if only he'd move on to actual digestion."

"How's Miki?" I asked as I dabbed ineffectually at the mess.

"Pretty much the same." He shrugged. "Maybe a bit better. It's hard to tell. She gave Boone part of a bottle yesterday, and at least she's come out of the depression chamber."

I laughed as much as his bad joke deserved and said, "She knows Ruth and Jane are coming, right?"

"Yeah. I told her. Her exact words were 'Whatever. I don't care.' Which aren't words I'm used to hearing from her, as you know."

Sarah N. Harvey

I laughed, since he seemed to be trying to make a joke, but it wasn't very funny. Miki's indifference was good for Ruth and Jane, but it still wasn't funny. Boone hiccuped in my arms, and I felt a different kind of dampness spread across my T-shirt.

"Want me to take him?" Dad asked. "I'm an ace diaperer."

"Me too," I replied. "Why don't you go have a shower? I'm going to clean Boone up, and then I'll check on Ruth. Jonah brought stuff to make fajitas, so just relax."

He nodded and ran his hand over Boone's head. "Relax, huh? I'll give it a shot. See you later, little guy," he said. "You're in good hands."

MIKI WOULDN'T JOIN us for dinner even though she loves fajitas; when Dad brought her tray back down, it looked as if she had picked at the chicken and ignored everything else, even her favorite hot sauce.

I finished burping Boone, changed him and took him up to bed. He slept beside Dad's side of the bed, in a super-cute bassinet with a Bert and Ernie theme. Miki was sitting up in bed, watching TV. Miki hates TV. Especially reality TV.

"Hey, Julia," she said. "Check this out." She pointed at the screen. "They're swimming in a vat of leeches."

I put Boone in his bassinet and covered him with a soft flannel blanket. The room smelled, as Ruth would say, like ass. A half-empty bottle of Shiraz sat on the night table.

I sat on the edge of the bed and watched a heavily tattooed, big-breasted woman in a bikini lower herself into the vat. Gross. I didn't know what to say. The woman in the bed didn't look at all like the woman my dad had married. For a start, she was really skinny and her breath was rank. Her skin was pale and flaky. Her teeth were yellow. Her nails were bitten. Her lips were chapped. The shadows under her eyes looked like spilled ink. In fact, she looked as if she had barely survived a dip in a vat of leeches. That whole new-mother glow that was illuminating Ruth seemed to have bypassed Miki altogether. I didn't get it. Miki had everything—money, a loving husband, a great job, a fabulous house. Ruth had nothing. It didn't make sense. Was it all just a big hormonal crapshoot?

"We missed you at dinner, Miki," I finally said. "Ruth's here, with Jane. I, um, wanted to thank you for taking them in. Our place is so small and—"

"I know. Your dad told me. He says Jane's adorable, and Ruth's a great mom." Her eyes filled with tears and she turned away from me and burrowed under the covers. I stroked her leg and watched her back shudder. I couldn't think of anything more to say. After a while she and Boone both seemed to be asleep, so I turned off the TV and tiptoed out of the room. As I was leaving, a faint and sorrowful voice wafted from the bed. "When something is wrong with my baby," Miki sang, "something is wrong with me." It was kind of backward, but I knew what she meant.

Twelve

When he was nearly thirteen, my brother Jem got his arm badly broken at the elbow.

—Harper Lee, *To Kill a Mockingbird*

I would have liked to name Ruth's baby Scout, after the main character in *To Kill a Mockingbird*, but Demi Moore and Bruce Willis scooped me, and I wouldn't want anyone to think that I named a baby after a celebrity's kid. I also toyed with the name Harper, but in the end, Jane just suited her better. Don't ask me why. Something about her eyes, maybe. It would be amazing if she ended up writing one of the greatest novels of all time, like Harper Lee, but I sure hope she turns out to be a bit more outgoing. I mean, Harper Lee wrote this one great book and then—nothing. She hung around with Truman Capote while he wrote *In Cold Blood*, and she won the Pulitzer Prize, but she never published another novel and she never gives interviews. I'm not even sure she's alive. How sad is that? Maybe I'll never write another word after I finish this book, but I'm pretty sure that no short guy with a lisp and bad taste in hats will ever replace Ruth as my best friend. And you can be damn sure that, if this book becomes a bestseller, I'll be selling the movie rights to the highest bidder, giving interviews to *Vanity Fair* and *Rolling Stone* and going to as many red-carpet events as possible. Ruth will be my date, and I will name my first son Atticus because by then I'll be a celebrity and Demi and Bruce will be old news. Maybe they could play Ruth's parents in the movie.

Two days after Ruth moved in at my dad's, someone banged on the front door and I opened it to find Pete and Peggy on the doorstep, Bibles in hand (I kid you not), flecks of foam on their lips. Okay, I'm exaggerating a bit about the foam, but it wasn't long before Pete was frothing at the mouth in the living room, where Ruth was nursing Jane in Dad's favorite brown leather recliner, the only evidence of his former bachelor existence. I perched on the arm of the chair, ready to take Jane upstairs if things got ugly, which seemed inevitable. Peggy didn't say anything; she just cleared a space on the love seat opposite Ruth and fixed her gaze on her granddaughter.

"Cover yourself," Pete barked as he shielded Peggy's eyes from the sight of Ruth's bare breasts. Peggy swatted his hand away and continued to stare at Jane. "Have you no shame? No sense of decency? Who is the father of this child?"

Pete continued in classic Pastor Pete style. He remained standing, looming over us like a trailer park prophet in his Wal-Mart jeans and stained white wifebeater. Talk about no sense of decency. "Who planted the demon seed in your tender young womb?"

Ruth laughed, which was probably unwise. "Johnny Appleseed," she said.

"You think this is funny?" Pete roared. "You dare to mock me?" Jane stopped nursing and swiveled her head toward the noise.

"Pete," Peggy whispered, tugging at his hand. "You promised." She continued to stare at Jane the way an anorexic looks at a piece of fudge cake—with adoration and disgust.

Pete glared at Peggy. "Tell me," he hissed, "on that baby's innocent soul. Tell me the father's name."

"I don't know," Ruth said. Peggy gasped and Pete lowered himself down beside her on the love seat.

"You don't know?" he said. "How can you not know?" As the answer dawned on him, he lowered his head and brought the Bible to his lips.

"That's right, Dad. There was more than one guy. And I don't care. Even if I did know, I wouldn't tell you. JJ's mine. Not his, not yours. Mine."

Pete shook his head as if a wasp was strafing him. "I don't believe you," he said. "You're just trying to protect him.

Tell me his name. If you marry him, the baby's soul will be saved. You can come home with us, and the baby will be raised to walk the path of righteousness. We'll see to that. I promise you."

Ruth shook her head vehemently. "The baby's name is Jane, Dad. Jane Julia Walters. And we're not coming home. Even if I knew who the father was, I wouldn't marry him. And as far as the path of righteousness goes—I've been down that path, and this is where it led me."

When Ruth said Jane's full name, I couldn't stop grinning, which made Pete even angrier. He looked as if he was going to have a stroke. His face was the color of borscht, and sweat was beaded on his upper lip. "I wash my hands of you, harlot," he said. "I have done all I can." He stood up, towering over his wife. "We have no daughter; we have no granddaughter. You and your child will burn in the eternal fires of hell. On your head be it."

"Pete," Peggy whimpered as he yanked her to her feet.

Ruth remained in the recliner, eyes shiny with tears. Her freckles stood out on her pale cheeks like cinnamon sprinkles on cappuccino foam. "Mom?" she said in a small voice. "Don't you even want to hold her?"

Peggy pulled away from Pete and moved toward Ruth, but Pete was too fast for her. He grabbed her elbow and hauled her toward the door. "Wife, submit yourself unto your husband," he yelled as he dragged her out of the house.

The sound of her sobs lingered in the air and performed a sad duet with Ruth's own.

Ruth switched Jane to her other breast, and we sat together as Jane suckled and Ruth cried. I missed the old Ruth—the one who would have yelled at her father and thrown a lamp at his head. I massaged Ruth's neck and wondered what it would feel like to have a father who was so full of hatred and a mother who was ignorant and weak. Ruth had always treated her parents like quaint relics of a bygone age or strange members of a tribe whose customs were, at worst, mystifying and, at best, amusing, but this was way past mystifying, and it sure wasn't amusing. If it was me, I'd probably become bitter and twisted, so it totally took me by surprise when Ruth stopped crying, blew her nose on the edge of the receiving blanket and said, "I feel so sorry for her."

"Jesus, Ruth. Why?"

"She's a prisoner. You saw the way she was looking at JJ?"

"Yeah."

"She wants to help—I can see it in her eyes—but she's been brainwashed."

"Maybe," I said. "But she's still an asshole."

"Don't call her that," Ruth said, sounding more like her old dangerous self. "I can call her that, but you can't. She'll find a way to see me. Maybe not right now, but when Dad calms down…"

"You could be right," I said. "I hope you are." When hippos fly, I thought.

Ruth stood up and handed Jane to me to burp. For some reason I had become the go-to burper in the house. Dad called me the Belch Whisperer. All my clothes were stained and sour-smelling, but I didn't care. It was my badge of courage.

"Don't be such a Jem," Ruth said as she buttoned up her shirt.

"A what?"

"A Jem—you know—Scout's brother in *To Kill a Mockingbird*. He got all bent out of shape about all the evil in the world. Don't be like that. It doesn't help."

I was stunned. "You actually read *To Kill a Mockingbird*?" I asked. To the best of my knowledge, the last book Ruth had read voluntarily was *The Poky Little Puppy*, which she liked because there were pictures of rice pudding and strawberry shortcake.

"Yeah," she replied. "I knew it was, like, your favorite book and I wanted to see what the deal was."

"And?"

"And I get it. I'm not an idiot. So can we stop talking about it and get something to eat? I'm always starving after Jane feeds."

"Okay," I said. "And Ruth?"

"Yeah?"

"Thanks."

"For what?" she asked.

"For the second J."

"You deserve it," she said. "So *now* will you call her JJ?"

"Not a chance," I said.

Ruth rolled her eyes and threw a cushion at my head.

RUTH'S FIRST VISITORS, after her parents, were Maria and Mark. He and I sat on the deck outside the dining room, sipping Pepsi and dipping chips into a big bowl of Maria's homemade salsa, while she checked out both sets of mothers and babies.

"So, Mom says you did a great job delivering Jane. It's pretty cool, huh?"

I nodded, my mouth full of chips, and he continued, "I used to help my mom out all the time, but when I hit puberty, some of her 'ladies' got a little weirded out with having me around. Guess they didn't want me looking at their, uh…"

"Snatches?" Ruth said as she joined us, cradling Boone in her right arm and clutching a baby monitor in her other hand.

Mark blushed and stood up. "I should get going," he mumbled.

"Not so fast," Ruth said, handing Boone to Mark. "Make yourself useful. Jane's asleep, but it's burp time for Boone.

Miki actually fed him today, but she hates burping him for some reason. I didn't want to push it."

I stood back to watch Mark's technique, which involved a lot of hip swiveling (it looked like the samba), accompanied by clockwise patting. Boone usually held out for at least ten minutes before he projectile-vomited all over me, but Mark was obviously an old pro—Boone delivered the goods in record time, with no accompanying gush of formula. Maybe it was a guy thing. Mark held Boone up in front of him, grinned and said, "Way to go, buddy. Lookin' good." Boone smiled, and I felt a trickle of jealousy run down my spine. I'd rather be spit up on any day.

"I'll take him now," I said, holding out my arms.

Mark blew a juicy raspberry on Boone's tummy, wrinkled his nose and said, "Good, 'cause I don't do diapers. See you ladies later."

The next visitor was Brandy, who came armed with candy and gossip. Ruth devoured both. I'm not sure which she enjoyed more. Maybe the candy, but it was a close call. Apparently everyone from school knew that Ruth had had a baby, which didn't surprise me. All Mark had to do was tell one person. Before too long, kids were passing around some really insane stuff: Ruth had had triplets, the delivery had taken place inside a pentangle under a full moon, the baby was black. The best one, which Rachel Greaves circulated, was that I had performed an emergency C-section with a steak knife and had stitched Ruth up with fishing line. Ruth thought the rumors were hilarious. I thought none of them were as unbelievable or even as interesting as the truth.

"Tell them I weigh three hundred pounds and my hair has fallen out," she told Brandy. "Tell them the baby's father is an albino circus dwarf. Tell them I fucked an alien and gave birth in a UFO."

"Tell them the truth," I suggested to Brandy. "She got pregnant the first time she had sex, her baby was delivered by her best friend, her parents kicked her out, the baby's beautiful and Ruth's an awesome mother."

Ruth rolled her eyes. "What's wrong with you, Jules?" she said. "Tell them I've converted to Kabbalah and Madonna is my real mom," she told Brandy. "Tell them anything you like."

"I'll do my best," Brandy said, "but it'll be hard to top the albino circus dwarf thing. Who is the father, anyway?"

"Nobody," Ruth said. "Just a guy."

STEWART AND MARSHALL turned up one night and made dinner for everybody. It was Miki's first meal with us since Ruth had moved in, and she only came downstairs because Stewart lured her with the promise of a vodka martini (straight up with a twist) and a floor show. I don't know if it was the vodka or the fact that a teenage Korean Dean

Martin look-alike delivered the invitation that got her out of bed. I guess it doesn't really matter, although I think it hurt my dad's feelings. He'd been trying to tempt her downstairs for weeks. Maybe if he'd dressed up like Sammy Davis Jr. and promised to sing "Candy Man" she would have come down sooner. Who knows? The important thing was that she joined us.

The dinner was fifties-themed and tasty in a kind of gross, over-processed way: Tang, Chex mix, onion dip, tuna and potato chip casserole, iceberg lettuce with Thousand Island dressing, and Bananas Foster for dessert. After dinner Stewart and Marshall did a Martin and Lewis routine that had everybody pissing their pants. Even Miki, who ordinarily acted like she'd had her funny bone surgically removed. Ruth laughed at all the jokes, but she kept telling everyone to keep it down so that we wouldn't wake the babies. Miki lay on the couch, martini in hand, and guffawed loudly at everything Stewart and Marshall said. It was like being in an old *Twilight Zone* episode where two women switch personalities after their babies are born. It freaked me out. I wanted the old Ruth back—the one who gnawed her fingernails until they bled and once took a dump on center ice at the hockey rink. She really hates hockey, and she wanted to see how long it took for shit to freeze. I even wanted the old Miki back—the one who bit the heads off interns and would never in a million years laugh at an anti-Semitic joke. Boone and Jane slept through it all in a playpen in the dining room. I was saying goodbye to Stewart and Marshall at the front door when Boone started to cry. Dad was in the kitchen cleaning up and Ruth was in the bathroom. Miki was already halfway up the stairs. She hesitated, turned and came back down. Slowly. She stood over Boone for a minute before she plucked him out of the playpen and headed for the kitchen.

Things were looking up.

JONAH CAME OVER a lot, but we didn't have a lot of time alone. Even so, I shaved my legs every day, worked on my tan, did a hundred sit-ups every morning, listened to creepy jazz and made him his favorite banana–chocolate chip muffins. But he still spent all his time with the only female in the house who shit herself on a regular basis and didn't know the difference between Monk and Miles.

"I'm going to be gone soon, Julia," he said one day in late August as we sat outside with Jane in the shade of the plum tree. Ruth was feeding Boone inside, and Miki was sleeping. Dad had gone back to work. It was as alone as we got.

"I know," I said, hoping he was going to profess his undying love for me. Jane was lying on her back, gurgling and waving her arms and legs like a doodlebug. A really cute doodlebug in a Baby Gap T-shirt. Jonah stretched out beside her on the blanket and rubbed her tummy. She burped and he laughed. Maybe I was missing something. I took a big gulp of my iced tea and belched loudly. Jonah looked up at me and frowned.

"Oops," I said. "My bad." I thought I looked and sounded adorable. I also wondered if I was losing my mind.

"S'okay," Jonah said as he turned back to Jane. No "Wait for me"; no "Run away to Vancouver with me." I glared at the back of his head for a few minutes before I got up and stomped into the house. For the first time ever, I wanted to punch him instead of kiss him.

"What's up with you and Jonah?" Ruth asked from the recliner.

"Nothing," I said. "He's just reminded me that he's leaving. As if I could forget." I started to unload the dishwasher, slamming the plates into the cupboard, hurling the knives and forks into a drawer.

"Why are you being such a selfish jerk?" said Ruth.

"I'm being a jerk?" I squeaked. "What about him?"

"He's leaving, Julia. As in going away and not coming back. It's a pretty big deal. The last thing he needs is a girlfriend back home messing things up for him."

"You think that's what I'll do—mess things up for him?"

"Yeah—in a way."

"What way?" I demanded. "It can't be any worse than what you've done. Talk about messing things up."

Ruth shrugged and shifted Boone onto her shoulder. "That's different. We're family. He'll get used to being away from us. You're way more distracting."

I laughed. Me—distracting. Studious, sensible Julia Riley, *femme fatale*.

"So I guess I can take that as a compliment, huh?" I said. "I'm so hot he can't concentrate?"

"Something like that."

"Well, it's bullshit and it's so not your business."

She shrugged again and stood up. "He's my brother, Jules. What can I say? I want what's best for him."

"Like I don't?" I yelled.

"Don't yell in front of the baby," Ruth said. Since when was she such a self-righteous bitch?

"I'll yell if I like. Give him to me. You know he likes me to burp him."

"Not when you're upset. Babies pick up on vibes."

All of a sudden I couldn't take it anymore. Nothing was turning out the way I had planned. I had no boyfriend, my best friend had turned into a Stepford mommy, my half-brother puked on me every chance he got, my zombie step-mother had abandoned all pretense of personal hygiene, and my dad was too worried about his wife and new kid to give his first-born child a second thought. I had no future with

Jonah. My little fantasy of sharing an apartment with Ruth in New York had crashed and burned. There were no survivors. I had no future. Period.

"I'm going home," I said stiffly. "Tell Jonah goodbye for me."

I kissed Boone's cheek. "Bye, little guy," I whispered. "Be good."

I grabbed my pack and walked home. The one person in the world I wanted to see was reading on our tiny balcony. She looked up and smiled as I came in. I burst into tears and she stood up and put her arms around me. She smelled like vanilla with a slight hint of bleach, which was a lot better than rancid baby vomit and dirty diapers, but it made me cry even harder. I'm not a pretty crier. Rivers of snot gushed out my nose; my mouth opened in a wail of despair. She stroked my hair and rocked me in her arms just the way she did when I was ten years old and Kelly Sims didn't invite me to her birthday party. We stood swaying on the balcony until my sobs subsided to pathetic gasping moans. She staggered slightly under my weight, and I hiccuped and stepped back, wiping my nose on the sleeve of my T-shirt. Her blouse was damp, but otherwise she looked the way she always does: neat, composed, hyper-alert. It takes a lot more than snot to phase my mother. I'd never really appreciated that before.

"Rough day at the baby farm?" she asked.

I nodded and sniffled a bit more. "Ruth and I need a break from each other. She's just so full of herself. Like having a baby makes her better than me or something. I mean, Jane's alive because of me. Ruth would have had an abortion if I hadn't helped her. And now she's all, like… super-maternal and shit." I stopped and took a breath. My mother looked bemused but attentive. "And Miki, well, Miki's just nuts." Mom's right eyebrow rose. I'd fill her in later, but I doubted news of Miki's incompetence would give Mom any joy. She's just not like that. She's all *hate the sin, love the sinner, turn the other cheek, judge not lest ye be judged.* I was in a judgmental, hate-the-sinner, slap-the-bitch mode. "I need to go back to school," I continued. "Read some books without diagrams of the birth canal, get my life back. Graduate. Date. Go to parties. Think about a career. Ruth's on her own. Jonah too. I'm out."

"Okay," Mom said. She didn't argue with me or ask me questions or even tell me things would get better. She didn't appear to be awaiting divine guidance. She just patted my cheek and asked me what I wanted for dinner. I was so glad to be home.

Thirteen

I am always drawn back to places where I have lived,
the houses and their neighborhoods.
— Truman Capote, *Breakfast at Tiffany's*

I was a little hard on Truman Capote before. After all, he
wrote *Breakfast at Tiffany's*, which was made into an awesome
movie. I saw the movie first and then I read the book, which
is unusual for me. I still like the movie better. To start with,
Audrey Hepburn is totally gorgeous. Sure, her eyebrows
look like they were drawn on with a wide black felt marker
and her voice sounds like she's got a glob of peanut butter
stuck in her throat, but she's still seriously beautiful. My
mom wasn't allowed to watch *Breakfast at Tiffany's* when she
was a teenager. My Nana thought it might give my mom
ideas, which is so dumb. It's not like Holly Golightly's a
hooker in the hot pants, stiletto boots, blow-job-in-an-alley
sense of the word. In the book she says she's only had eleven
lovers—eleven rich lovers who adore her and pay for her

companionship, which may or may not include sex. They get amazing arm candy; she gets jewelry, designer gowns, a satin sleep mask and George Peppard for a best friend. The smooth, blond, tasty, pre-*A-Team* George Peppard. Some of the girls at school have had more than eleven lovers by the time they're sixteen, and yeah, I know, they're not getting paid for it, but still…everyone gets something out of the deal, even in high school. My mom and I have watched *Breakfast* together a few times, even though it's probably not on *Christianity Today's* Top Ten list. We pull on long gloves, douse ourselves in *4711* perfume, put our hair up in French twists and sing along to "Moon River." We always cry. It makes perfect sense to me that Paul and Holly love each other: they're both outsiders, even though Paul is sort of dull and Holly is, let's face it, a total wack job. Holly has friends with weird names—Sally Tomato, Rusty Trawler, Jose Ybarra-Jaeger. Paul has Holly. He gives her a St Christopher's medal; she gives him an empty birdcage. I could write you a ten-page paper on the significance of those gifts. Or on why Holly says, "I'd rather have cancer than a dishonest heart." I'm going to have that put on T-shirts and give them as Christmas gifts. And don't get me started on why Mickey Rooney was cast as Holly's Japanese neighbor, Mr. Yunioshi. That's just all kinds of wrong. Wars have been started over less.

The big difference between the movie and the book is that, in the book, the narrator (who never reveals his name)

and Holly are friends, not lovers. A lot of that has to do
with the narrator (and the author) being gay, but I like the
idea that people can love each other deeply without sex
messing it up. I thought about that a lot after I went back
to my mom's. I wondered if maybe that's the way Jonah
and I were headed. We'd never really had sex anyway, so
would it be so terrible to back off the whole thing and try
and be friends?

I WENT BACK to my old routine—Dad's house on Saturday,
church with Mom on Sunday, back to Dad's for dinner—
but Jonah was never there when I was, and he didn't call.
I missed seeing the babies all the time, and I really missed
Ruth, but every time I saw her she was busy with Jane, so
I spent my time with Miki and Boone. Miki had started
taking some kind of medication, and she didn't spend all
her time locked away in the decompression room anymore.
Maybe Ruth's Super-Mom routine had kick-started Miki's
competitive streak. Whatever it was, Miki was way better.
She still needed help with Boone, and she spent a lot of time
sleeping, but she fed him and changed his diapers and took
him for walks. Dad was thrilled.

"You girls ever going to make up?" Miki asked one day
when we were taking Boone for a walk in his bright orange
Bugaboo stroller (with uv-block parasol!). Trust Miki to buy

the Ferrari of strollers, although I have to admit, it's pretty cool. "Ruth seems kind of down," she added.

"She seems okay to me," I said. "She's always all 'Oh, I have to sterilize Boone's bottles' or 'I'm freezing a batch of organic applesauce for when the babies start on solid food.' Brandy's even offered to babysit so Ruth can go out for coffee with me, but Ruth's always got something more important to do, like clean Jane's ears or clip her fingernails. It's pretty obvious she doesn't want me around."

Miki stopped the stroller and turned to face me. "For a smart girl you can be pretty dumb sometimes, Julia." She was smiling when she said it, so I squelched my impulse to a) smack her and b) run away. "Ruth's just as confused and frightened as I was. She just doesn't want anyone to know it. Motherhood really messes with your head, whether you're seventeen or forty-two. Your world gets really tiny— and your body goes haywire. Look at me—I completely derailed. Some days I still need to go off by myself. Ruth's different. She loves looking after Jane and Boone, and she's really good at it, but I think she's lonely. She never wants to be by herself, not like I do. Think about it: her parents have cut her out of their lives like she's a malignant tumor, she isn't going back to school, her brother's leaving and her best friend is sulking. She has no skills, no way of earning money. All she has is Jane, who is totally dependent on her. Or at least that's the way it must feel to her. I don't mind

admitting that I'm pretty dependent on her too. If she and
Jane hadn't turned up I'd probably still be locked away in
the decompression room. She's scared, Julia. Wouldn't you
be?" She turned the stroller around and started walking back
to the house. I trailed after her.

"And as far as Jonah's concerned," Miki continued, "stop
feeling sorry for yourself. Since when do girls always have
to wait for the guy to call? It's not the nineteen-fifties. Pick
up the damn phone, Julia, before he leaves for Vancouver.
Anyone with eyes in their head can see he's crazy about you.
Everyone but you, apparently."

"But he's going away," I whined.

"Jesus, Julia, Vancouver's not Outer Mongolia. Get a grip."

And with that she took off at an almost-jog. I didn't
try to keep up (I hate jogging and I was wearing flip-flops
anyway), and when I got back to the house, I went straight
to the decompression room. I hung the *Do Not Disturb*
sign on the doorknob and climbed into the bed. I needed
to think.

After about an hour I had come to two conclusions.
First, Miki was probably right about everything, but I had to
prioritize. Ruth could wait, since she wasn't going anywhere.
Second, if Jonah blew me off, I was heading straight to the
Dairy Queen to bury myself in what I call "the full catas-
trophe meal": a Brownie Earthquake followed by a Pecan
Mudslide. And I was taking Ruth with me.

I snuck out of the decompression room and grabbed the portable phone off the coffee table. Technically, phones are forbidden in the quiet room, but there was no way I was phoning Jonah with Ruth around. I called Jonah's cell. It went straight to voice mail, and in my mind I could see him frowning at the screen and pressing *Ignore*. I burst into tears and hung up without leaving a message. I put the phone down and curled up in the fetal position on the bed. Ten minutes later, when the phone rang, I picked it up on the first ring. My hands were sweating.

"Hello?" I croaked.

"Julia?" Jonah's voice sounded shaky. Was it possible he was as nervous as me? "You called? Is everything okay?"

"Not really," I said. "I mean, Ruth and Jane are fine, if that's what you want to know."

He was silent for a moment, a moment in which I abandoned hope. When he finally spoke, all he said was, "I'm coming over."

"What? No!" I yelped into the phone, but he had already hung up. I was screwed. The boy I loved was coming over, and I was hiding in a small dark room, wearing a pair of my mom's baggy, pleat-front, Eddie Bauer khaki shorts and a faded Run for the Cure T-shirt circa 2002. I had hairy legs, dirty hair, chipped nail polish, chapped lips and probably bad breath. If Jonah saw me now, he'd break up with me for sure. And anyway, I wanted to look good when he broke up with me, on the off chance that he might eat his heart out later when I was on the cover of *People* magazine. I imagined him sitting in an overheated kitchen after a twelve-hour shift, holding the magazine up to his sous-chef and saying, with a catch in his voice, "You know, she could have been mine…" And I would come to his restaurant with my rich successful artist boyfriend, and Jonah would prepare our meal himself and serve us, with tears in his eyes…

Muffled voices interrupted my breakup fantasy before I got to the part where Jonah tells me that he made the biggest mistake of his life back when we were teenagers, and I smile pityingly and say…

"If the 'Do Not Disturb' sign is up, that's what it means. Unless there's a fire or something." Miki's voice was coming from right outside the door. I burrowed under the covers and closed my eyes.

"So let's light one. She's been in there for, like, three hours. It's not like her. What if she's, like, choked on her own vomit or something, like Janis Joplin?" Ruth sounded really worried, which was sweet, but I hoped Miki realized that there was a chance Ruth wasn't speaking figuratively about lighting a fire. For all I knew, she was piling rolled-up newspapers outside the door and reaching for the matches. I smiled a bit in the dark. Maybe the old Ruth wasn't completely gone. Maybe she needed me after all, if only to keep her from doing stupid things like burning Dad's house down.

"Why on earth would she be choking on her own vomit?" Miki asked sharply. "She hasn't been drinking, has she?"

"I really need to see if she's okay, Dr. Stevens." Jonah's voice was low and insistent. "If she wants me to go, I'll go. I promise."

There was a soft knock on the door, followed by Miki's voice.

"Jonah's here to see you, Julia. Can he come in?"

"Okay," I said. "But no lights."

The door opened, and Jonah stumbled into the room.

He groped his way to the bed, stubbing his toe on the chair.

"Shit," he said. I couldn't help it—I giggled. He sat on the edge of the bed, and I stuck my head out from under the duvet. No way he was going to see what I was wearing if I could help it.

"I'm leaving tomorrow, Julia," he said. "I wanted to see you before I went."

"Tomorrow?" I squeaked. "So soon?"

"Yeah. I gotta get set up before classes start. Meet my roommates, buy my books."

"Oh."

"But I have to tell you something before I go."

"Okay." Here it comes, I thought. The big *It's not you, it's me—I've found someone else—You're too immature for me* speech. I held my breath and dove back under the covers. I wished I could choke on my own vomit. I'd never heard of anyone choking to death on tears and snot.

"This has been the best summer of my life," Jonah said slowly. "You, me and Ruth at the lake. Jane's birth. But mostly you. You're amazing—the way you've helped Ruth, the way you commit to things, even really crazy things. The way you giggle when you're nervous—I should have said something sooner, but I knew I was going away and it didn't seem fair to you. Long-distance relationships are hard…and you probably want to date guys your own age and chefs have such brutal hours—"

"Are you kidding?" I screeched, flinging off the blankets and throwing my arms around him. "Boys my own age are losers. And we can text all the time and talk on the phone and visit on holidays." I started kissing him—his perfect chin, his crooked nose, his chiseled cheekbones, finally his delicious lips. "It's only for a year," I mumbled into his mouth. "I mean, how hard can it be?"

Jonah laughed, and I pulled him down on the bed beside me. A knock on the door reminded me that Ruth and Miki were probably still standing outside, with their ears pressed against the door.

"Everything okay in there?" Miki asked.

"Couldn't be better," I yelled.

"You coming out anytime soon?" Ruth sounded aggrieved and slightly dangerous, the way she did when

Jonah and I played Scrabble or watched public television. I grinned at Jonah and rubbed my nose against his.

"Ahhh. An Inuit kiss," he sighed. "Can't say Eskimo anymore, you know." He loomed over me in the dark and I felt his eyelashes graze my cheek. A butterfly kiss. Nobody had given me a butterfly kiss since I was about six.

"We'd better get out of here before Ruth goes all Chuck Norris on us," he said. "You know how she gets."

"That I do," I said. I got off the bed, yanked down my T-shirt, smoothed my shorts and ran my fingers through my hair. There wasn't much I could do about the way I looked but suddenly it didn't matter anymore. Jonah held out his hand to me and we left the decompression chamber together. I took the *Do Not Disturb* sign off the door. I didn't think I'd need it for a while.

JONAH LEFT FOR Vancouver the next day, and after that I kept super-busy. Now that I was officially his girlfriend, I missed him more than I ever had when he was away at Bible boot camp. School was about to start up again. I dropped by Dad's every day to see the babies, but I came home every night to have dinner ready for my mom when she got back from work. I'm not much of a cook, so it was nothing fancy—lots of salads and grilled fish or chicken—and once in a while we even had dessert, which was a totally new thing for my mom.

"Are you sure you're not getting too thin?" she asked me one evening as we were doing the dishes together.

I laughed. "Not a chance," I said. "I never thought I'd hear you say those words, though."

"I know, I know," she said. "Sometimes I get a little, um, obsessive."

"Just a little," I replied. I bumped her bony hip with my own, and she flicked the dishcloth at my butt.

"I like being this weight," I told her, "but I don't want to get any skinnier. Ruth and I are sort of trying to keep each other honest, and it helps that she can't eat spicy food or chocolate while she's nursing. She's had to cut down on her caffeine intake too, which means no caramel mochaccinos. She's kind of bummed about that. So that pretty much means I don't have those things either. Solidarity and all that. Plus, neither of us has any money, so the occasional tub of vanilla Häagen-Dazs is about as exciting as it gets."

"So you guys are getting along a bit better these days?" she asked.

"Yeah, we're good." I hesitated. I wanted to talk about Miki—how she'd helped me see that Ruth was struggling with being a mother even though she acted like she had it all figured out. I wanted to tell her how much I loved Boone. I was tired of pussyfooting around in both houses. Maybe if I told Mom how messed up Miki had been, she'd lighten up.

"How come you hate Miki so much?" I blurted out.

"I don't hate Miki," she said. "Why would you think that?"

"Oh, I don't know, let's see: she's got your husband, a new baby, a lot of money, a fabulous house and a great job."

"So—let me get this straight—I'm supposed to hate her for having a good life?" She smiled and put her hands together as if she was praying. "That wouldn't be very Christian of me, would it?"

I was gobsmacked. She was making a joke about Jesus. What would be next—a T-shirt that said *Jesus Loves You (but only as a friend)*? "Well, don't you hate her? Isn't that why you freak out every time Dad calls or comes by? Isn't that why you haven't bought a baby present for Boone?"

"Oh, sweetie," she sighed. "Is that what you think? That I'm jealous of Miki?"

When I nodded, she put down the dishcloth, sat down at the kitchen table and pointed at the other chair.

"Sit," she said. "This is hard to explain, and you'll probably think I'm crazy, but here goes." She took a deep breath. "It's not jealousy or hatred I have the problem with—it's love. I've loved your dad since I was your age, but I've known for a long time that we weren't good together. We were," she frowned while she searched for the word, "combustible. He's my addiction and my faith is my AA. You were too young to remember, but we fought a lot and he hated it when I became a Christian. You want a definition of irony, here it is: the thing that finally drove us apart—my faith—is what keeps me from hating him and Miki. But I try really hard to stay out of his life, which unfortunately means staying out of Miki's and now Boone's life too. I thought it was best for everybody—including you—if I didn't get involved. At all. Ever. And sure, sometimes I'm a bit jealous, but only of the material things—the house, the cars, the vacations. Which brings me to something else I need to talk to you about."

There was more? All this time I thought Mom hated Dad and Miki, when she's actually more like a recovering alcoholic who can't go near a bar? Yikes. What was next? Had the Internet spit up a Bible-believing rancher boyfriend in Texas or somewhere else I really didn't want to go? Wasn't this backward? Wasn't I the one who was supposed to be freaking her out? And wasn't she the one who taught me all about self-control and self-discipline? I must have looked terrified, because she laughed and grabbed my hand as I got up to pace the kitchen.

"Sit down, Julia. It's not that bad. I'm going back to school in a couple of weeks. I should have told you sooner, but everything was so…hectic."

"You're going back to school? What for?" I had a sudden vision of my mom, in her favorite red and white snowflake sweater and sensible walking shoes, sitting next to me in my math class, joining the choir, playing field hockey, pulling straight A's.

"I have to do some upgrading at the college first. Then I'm going to apply to law school as a mature student. One of the partners at the firm has been after me for years to get off my butt and go for it. He's got some pull at the university, and he's written me an amazing letter of recommendation. I can work part-time if I like, but I'll probably get student loans and try to get through as quickly as possible. Of course, I have to get into law school first, but Gary thinks I'll be fine as long as I score high on the LSAT. He's helping me with that too."

Gary? Who was Gary, and why was my mom blushing? I was speechless, and believe me, that doesn't happen very often. A career change is one thing, but a lawyer boyfriend? Maybe Texas wasn't such a bad idea.

"Julia?" my mom said. "Say something, honey. I know it's a bit of a shock, but I'm not getting any younger. And let's face it, I probably already know more law than most of the lawyers in my firm." She laughed and got up from the table, kissing the top of my head on her way to the living room.

I sat for a few minutes and tried to digest everything she'd told me: new career, possibly a new boyfriend—Mom was getting on with her life. So were Jonah and Ruth and Dad and Miki. I sat down beside her on the couch and laid my head on her shoulder.

"So, this Gary guy—is he hot?" I said.

Fourteen

All this happened, more or less.
—Kurt Vonnegut, *Slaughterhouse-Five*

I didn't scribble an outline in crayon on some wallpaper before I started writing this book, as Vonnegut says he did. I didn't actually write an outline at all. I just sat down and wrote. As you've probably noticed, there are no aliens (unless you count Ruth's parents) in my book, and the only wars I've ever witnessed are domestic ones, which don't have quite the narrative punch of the firebombing of Dresden. Even so, when I was writing I often felt like Billy Pilgrim, Vonnegut's hero, looping around in time, dropping in on my own life. Nobody can top Vonnegut when it comes to mixing up tragedy, fantasy, memoir and comedy. He makes it all seem perfectly reasonable. Which it is. Nobody's life is all one way—tragic, comic, fantastic—it's all just a big spicy jambalaya of absurdity, even without visitors from the planet Tralfamadore.

My mom and I both went back to school the week after she told me about Gary. It feels weird, being at school without Ruth, as if I'd forgotten one of my legs at home. Very destabilizing. We've been going to the first day of school together forever, clutching new HB pencils and pristine notebooks, our hair held in place by matching Strawberry Shortcake barrettes. I'm in a new homeroom, with Stewart sitting to my right and Brandy right behind him. Marshall's in another classroom, which is just as well. Over the summer, Stewart and Brandy hooked up, and Dino and Jerry are no more. Marshall's pretty pissed. He's even dropped out of the Classics Club, so we let Mark Grange join. Turns out he's a total movie freak. He even has this thing that he calls Hollywood 9-1-1, which is a list of 555 phone numbers from movies and television shows. So you can call, say, Mr. Burns from *The Simpsons* or the Christian Broadcasting Channel from *South Park*.

For the first couple of weeks of school I answered so many questions about Ruth and Jane that I thought my head was going to explode. I finally did up a FAQ sheet and handed it out to anyone who approached me with a question. *Who's the father?* was the question on most girls' glossy lips; a lot of guys asked, *What does it feel like to have your hand up your best friend's, uh, you know?* Neither concern was addressed on my FAQ sheet. A simple *Mind your own effing business* sufficed. Then Ruth brought Jane to school

one afternoon. She was immediately surrounded by a gaggle
of cooing girls (including that bitch Rachel Greaves, who
had started the rumor about the steak-knife caeserean),
and a bunch of guys who muttered things like *Look at her
tits* and *She's hot, man,* as they gave each other high fives.
Rick Greenway was nowhere to be seen. After Ruth's visit
my celebrity status decreased dramatically, especially when
a rumor started going around about the home ec teacher's
passionate affair with a German shepherd. It turned out
she'd fallen in love with a man of German descent who owns
a sheep farm in New Zealand, but even so, I wasn't in the
spotlight anymore, which suited me fine.

"SO, IS RUTH, like, Boone's live-in nanny now?" Mark asked
me as we were walking over to my dad's house after school
one day. Mark came over a lot. He was a genius with the
babies when he could drag himself away from staring at
Ruth's boobs. When Mark was around, everybody laughed
a lot, especially Miki. He was like a long-lost second cousin
from a branch of the family that had been disowned because
of unwise marriages to unreliable Spaniards. Not that Maria
was unreliable—quite the opposite. Mark's dad, whereabouts
unknown, was definitely the unreliable one.

"Yup," I replied. "That's the deal. She helps Miki
with Boone and she gets free room and board. And get

this—Miki's homeschooling her. And she's getting good grades. Better than she ever did at school."

"Wow. That means she'll graduate at the same time as you, right?"

"I guess so. I'm hoping the school will let her come to our grad, but you know what tight-asses they can be."

"Yeah. I can't wait to get out of there."

"What are you going to do after you graduate?" I asked him. Mark was smart, straight-A smart. He could go to any university he wanted to, probably with a full scholarship. So could I, for that matter, if only I could decide where I wanted to go and what I wanted to do. I wasn't used to feeling so indecisive. The grand plan was undergoing a serious renovation. Who knew what would be left standing.

"Not sure yet. My mom wants me to be a doctor." He rolled his eyes. "It's such a cliché—my son the doctor."

I laughed. "Everyone thinks I should be a doctor too, but I don't know. I'm thinking midwife school. But don't tell anyone. I might still want to do creative writing. Or run a bookstore."

"My mom could help you with the midwife thing," Mark said.

"I know," I said. "But I'm not ready to commit to anything. It's all anyone wants to talk about. The school counselor, my parents, kids at school. Everyone acts like it's make or break in grade twelve. One wrong decision and you're wearing a dorky hat and asking 'Do you want fries with that?' for the rest of your life."

"I know," Mark said glumly. "I'm getting it already and I'm only in grade eleven."

We walked in silence for a few minutes. Just as we turned in to my dad's driveway, Mark asked, "Does your dad like his job?"

"Are you nuts? He looooves it," I said. "He used to be an ER nurse, but he burned out so he went back to school and took courses in neonatal nursing. He says it's the best thing he ever did. Career-wise, anyway. Why?"

"Just curious," Mark said as we walked in the front door.

When we got inside, Ruth greeted us wearing a red T-shirt emblazoned with the words *Get a Taste of Religion— Lick a Witch*.

"Like it?" she asked. "Miki gave it to me."

"Awesome," Mark said. "Where are the little dudes?"

"Sleeping in the playpen in the living room, so we gotta be quiet. And Jane's not a dude," said Ruth. "Miki's napping. Man, that chick sleeps a lot. Guess middle-aged motherhood has its downside."

She cackled softly and led us into the kitchen, where a huge cardboard box sat on the kitchen table.

"What's in the box?" I asked.

"I'm not sure. It was on the doorstep this morning when Miki went to get the paper," she said. "The box is from www.christislord.com, so I guess it's from my folks. It's probably all the junk from my old room. Installation One." She grimaced and absentmindedly massaged her right breast. Mark blushed, but he didn't look away. "I'm debating whether to unpack it or just store it and give it to Jane when she's older. What do you think?"

"Store," I said. "Definitely store."

"Open," Mark said.

"Thanks, guys. You're a lot of help."

I glared at Mark. "You don't know her parents. They probably burnt her stuff and shoveled the ashes into a box and pissed on it."

"Or maybe not," Mark said. "Maybe it's a...you know... peace offering.

I snorted and raised an eyebrow at Ruth. She shrugged and picked up a knife off the counter and started hacking at the packing tape. As she lifted the flaps of the box, I could see an envelope sitting on top of what looked like a blanket. Ruth lifted the letter out as if she expected it to explode. Letter-bombing your own daughter. That would be harsh even for Pastor Pete.

Her hands trembled as she tore the envelope open; it only took her a minute to read the enclosed letter. Whatever it said made her eyes fill with tears. She handed me the letter as she reached into the box and pulled out the blanket, which was pink and fluffy. "Read it," she said as she buried her face in the blanket. "Aloud." She was sobbing now, her shoulders heaving. Mark rubbed her back while I read the letter.

My dear Ruth,

Your father does not want me to contact you. He took everything out of your room and he was going to burn it but I managed to pack it up while he was at the Wednesday night prayer and pizza group. I have included some of your baby clothes and the baby blanket I crocheted when you were born. I think of you every day and I pray that you and Jane are well. I also pray that someday you will be able to forgive me. Then I will be able to forgive myself. Miracles can happen, you know.

In Jesus' blessed name,
Mom

"You were both right," Ruth said. "It's an almost-burnt offering." She giggled and put the blanket aside to rummage around in the box. Everything was packed carefully, lovingly even, between layers of pink tissue paper. All the baby clothes were pink, which made Ruth wince and laugh. "Now you know why I hate pink," she said as she held up a pair of OshKosh overalls. "But these are pretty darn cute, don't you think?"

"Not as cute as these," I said, unearthing a pair of tiny pink patent leather Mary Janes.

"What's up with this?" Mark asked. He was dangling the lacy orange thong from his index finger. Ruth grabbed it away from him and threw it back into the box.

"Wouldn't you like to know," she said. "It was another life, right, Julia?"

I nodded as she sealed the box and wrote on the side in black felt pen *Installation One: Childhood.* "I've already started *Installation Two*," she said. "Wanna see it? It's called *Motherhood* and it's gonna be wicked. Way better than number one."

She dragged us upstairs to her room, which was twice as big as her room at Pete and Peggy's. Big bay windows looked out over the backyard; Jane's crib was tucked into the bay, and the wall opposite the queen-size bed was covered by a giant corkboard. Stuck to the corkboard were a cord clamp, a photo of Ruth holding Boone and Jane, a letter from Jonah, a picture of Jonah in his white chef's outfit, a picture of Miki and Dad with Boone, a picture of my mom taken at my twelfth birthday (I could tell from the candles on the cake she was holding), two Ziploc bags—one holding microscopically small nail clippings, one containing wisps of hair—and a picture of me that was "framed" with feathers, glitter, a LifeSavers necklace and a red ribbon rosette that said *World Champion Best Friend* in gold script.

"Your dad put up the corkboard for me," she said as she stuck her mother's letter onto the board with a safety pin. "That way I won't ruin the walls. It's just a start, but it's pretty cool, huh?"

"Very cool," I said. The three of us sprawled on the bed and gazed at the wall in silence. I might have fallen asleep, but the babies started to whimper and Mark was up like a shot.

"I'll heat Boone's bottle," he said as he went out the door.

"Feeding time on the farm," Ruth sighed as she sat up. "You coming?"

"Is it okay if I stay up here for a bit?" I asked. "I'm kinda tired and you and Mark have the babies covered."

"Mark just wants to stare at my boobs," Ruth said, "but that's okay. No one else is gonna look at them for a while. Wanna go for a walk later?"

"Sure," I said. "I won't be long."

After she left, I got up and looked more closely at Installation Two. I reread Peggy's letter. I'd been wrong to tell Ruth not to open it, but then, she's used to me playing it safe. She always does what she wants, no matter what I say. I should be used to it by now. I'd been wrong about so many things in the last year, though. Wrong about Ruth, whom I never thought would take motherhood seriously. Wrong about my mom, who isn't naïve or ignorant or stupid.

Wrong about Miki, who finds motherhood way more challenging than med school. Wrong about my parents' relationship. I was even wrong about Peggy, I guess, although I still think we'll be doing double axels in hell before she breaks away from Pete. I'm not going to say that to Ruth, though.

I still don't think teenagers should be mothers. I really don't. Ruth just happens to be an exception to that rule. For a start, most teen moms don't get taken in by a singing nurse and a baby doctor who insists that homeschooling be taken very seriously. Most teen moms don't have a brother who phones every night, names cakes after his niece and looks yummy in a hat shaped like a giant mushroom. Most teen moms don't have friends like me and Mark and Brandy, who will babysit at the drop of a hat. I know that there are times when Ruth is tired and discouraged and fed up with endless diaper changing and vegetable pureeing, but it's not in her nature to brood about it. She's more likely to whip up a smoothie with leftover mashed bananas and call me up and beg me to come over and play *Pictionary* or watch crap TV. She always turns the TV off when the babies are in the room, though, even if we're in the middle of *Top Model*. No TV for the babies. That's one of Ruth's rules. She has almost as many rules as I used to have lists. It's like living in a parallel universe. A much happier parallel universe.

Ruth has started reading because it's something to do while she nurses Jane. I've given her all my favorite books, but she won't read anything by Dickens and she still thinks Jane Austen is a stuck-up priss. She really liked *Catch-22*, though, and I had to get her every single Vonnegut book from the library after she read *Slaughterhouse-Five*. Right now she's binge-reading Anne Rice vampire novels, which is actually kind of scary. I'm reading an awesome book called *The Poisonwood Bible* by Barbara Kingsolver. One of the characters is like Pastor Pete on crack. Absolutely nuts. Ruth's gonna love it. Or not. Hard to tell.

One of Ruth's rules is that Boone and Jane must be read to every day, without fail. *Goodnight Moon*, *Baby Beluga* (my dad's fave, for obvious reasons), *The Very Hungry Caterpillar*, *Peep-O*. Jane's attention span leaves something to be desired. She's like a gnat with ADD. Boone has all the makings of a serious reader, though. He furrows his little brow and bats at the pages with his pudgy paws. That's my bro. Jane's more into gnawing the corners and drooling. I've started making a library for them, although it will be a while before I can read them *Mr. Gumpy's Outing* or *The Wind in the Willows* or *The Lord of the Rings*. In the meantime, Ruth's fallen madly in love with Toad of Toad Hall, and she thinks Stuart Little is a blast in his little red convertible. But then, she's always liked guys with cool cars.

Another of Ruth's rules is that she, Miki, Dad, me and the babies must eat dinner together at least once a week. She also thinks we should have an extended family Christmas this year—Mom, Gary, Nana and me; Miki and Dad and Boone; Ruth and Jonah and Jane; Maria and Mark. I'm working on Mom. Ever since she started dating Gary, she's relaxed a bit around Dad. And Gary's an okay guy. Not terribly exciting, but I don't need an exciting step-father, if that's what he becomes. Boring is good, if he makes my mom happy. Miki and Dad are cool with anything we cook up (ha-ha) for Christmas, as long as Dad gets to sing cheesy Christmas carols (he and I do a smokin' rendition of "Baby, It's Cold Outside") and Miki gets to play charades. I happen to know that my mom kicks ass at charades, so I'm hoping the opportunity to act out *Faster Pussycat Kill! Kill!* will tip the scales in favor of the family Christmas.

In the meantime, I'm doing the whole long-distance thing with Jonah—e-mail, text messages, Facebook, phone calls, webcam, the occasional visit—which is a pain, since I'm trying to keep my grades up, and he can be *very* distracting. When we're together, it's awesome; when we're not, it sucks. Sometimes he gets on my nerves, especially when he won't shut up about his favorite knife or the best way to do a *chiffonade*, but most of the time I'm so busy I forget to miss him. Does that mean I don't love him? I don't know. Time will tell, I guess.

I'm still working at the bookstore a couple of evenings a week, saving all my money for when I leave home next year. Mom's surprisingly okay with me moving out.

Maybe it's because she won't have to sleep on the couch anymore. Or maybe she and Gary want to shack up together. Who knows? She's busy with school and happier than I've seen her in a long time. And she totally deserves it, even if it means I'm not the center of her universe anymore. I feel a bit like an astronaut floating through space, my only connection to my past a long thin cord of memories. As long as no one clamps the cord, I'll be okay.

I doubt whether Ruth and Jane will come with me when I leave. Ruth's really settled in at Dad's, and she's definitely not ready to tackle another big upheaval. And I don't think Miki could get by without her. I understand all that. What I don't understand is that she actually believes her mother is going to start acting like a regular mom and grandma. That's part of the reason she wants to stay where she is. She told me that she thinks that as long as she doesn't give up on Peggy, there's a chance Peggy won't give up on her. That equation makes sense to her for some reason.

Anyway, I try not to make elaborate plans anymore, especially elaborate plans for other people's lives. It's just too disappointing when things don't work out. I know Ruth thinks it's way more exciting not to have everything all planned out ahead of time, but my dad doesn't call me Little Miss Sobersides for nothing. Going with the flow isn't my natural state, although I have cut down on the obsessive list-making. The only lists I make these days are for groceries.

Like David Copperfield, I'm not sure if I'm the hero of my own life. Writing it all down has helped, but I still feel a little freaked out sometimes, like I'm the survivor of an emotional earthquake and I can't find my emergency supplies.

As I get to the end of this story, my fascination with first lines isn't much help to me. Now I keep thinking about last lines—aren't they just as important? Shouldn't a novel's last line sum up the book in a way that lingers (preferably like the scent of roses or chocolate chip cookies, not like a fart) in the reader's mind? When I look back over all the first lines I quoted and all the books they were taken from, I realize there's actually a theme, a connecting motif, as Mrs. Hopper would say. Which is kind of crazy, since I chose the quotes because they were from books I love, not because they were part of some Julia Riley literary grand plan. Really. But sometimes things just work out, whether you make a plan or not. So I'm not going to tell you what the theme is—if you don't figure it out, it doesn't really matter. It's just a story. My true story. And yes, there will be a test.

Sarah N. Harvey is an editor and the author of *Puppies on Board*, *The West Is Calling* (with Leslie Buffam) and *Bull's Eye*, an Orca Soundings. She lives in Victoria, British Columbia, with a combative fish named Yul.